REEF OF DEATH

PAUL ZINDEL

HYPERION PAPERBACKS FOR CHILDREN

New Y

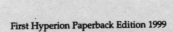

First Hyperion Paperback Edition 1999

For information address Hyperion Books for Children,
114 Fifth Avenue, New York, New York 10011-5690.
Printed in the United States of America.
5 7 9 10 8 6
Library of Congress Cataloging-in-Publication Data
Zindel, Paul.
Reef of Death / Paul Zindel
p. cm.
Summary: While helping a beautiful Aboriginal girl search for her people's
missing treasure near the Great Barrier Reef, seventeen-year-old PC finds
himself fighting an evil scientist and a deadly underwater monster.
ISBN 0-7868-1309-1 (pbk.)
[1. Monsters-Fiction. 2. Great Barrier Reef (Qld.)-Fiction. 3. Australia-Fiction.
4. Australian Aborigines-Fiction. 5. Buried treasure-Fiction. 6. Adventure
and adventurers-Fiction.] I. Title.
PZ7.Z647Rh 1998
[Fic]-dc21
97-21864

To my editor, Robert O. Warren
who makes certain that kids always win . . .

ACKNOWLEDGMENTS

To the students of DeWitt Middle School, Michigan—thanks for your help with the title.

Also, much appreciation to the many librarians and teachers who shared their generous thoughts and inspiring students with me during the writing of this book. Special thanks to Edna L. Hussey of Ka Hui Heuhelu, Hawaii; Sue Spaniol, Cindy Dobrez, Lynn Rutan, Sue Hornbach, Clare Howell, and all my other friends in Michigan; thanks to Patricia Sonnet, Bandana, and all the students at the American Embassy School, New Delhi, India; to my friends Louise Rosario, Kevin Rose, Julie Rusnak, Susan King-Lachance, and all the kids at Jakarta International School; to Debbie Pettid and her patrons; Vivian Ellner and her students at the United Nations International School; Wendy Kosterman; Judy Transue; Roberta Long and her dynamic students at the University of Alabama at Birmingham; Ruth Davis and the terrific kids at the Wellsburg Middle School in West Virginia; Lynn Lello; Peggy Schmidt; Judith Horowitz; Carol Rhodes; Pat Shea-Bishoff; Sandra Payne; Lillian Hruska; Nancy Rosner; Gracelyn Fina Shea of the Texas Library Association; Kathleen Miksis and all my new friends in Reading, Massachusetts; Ellen Rubin, Jane Duval, Teri Lesesne, Spencer Manley Ellis and his students; and to Catherine Balkin and Patty Aitken.

CONTENTS

REEF OF DEATH

The creature swam in the blackness at the base of the reef, ganglia rising out of its head like glistening, dead eels. It moved gracefully between the white underwater cliff and a world of sulfurous mounds—each the size of a football stadium. The volcanic mounds had been violently exploded up through the ocean floor more than 50,000 years ago—and they were still growing. Towering chimneys shot out minerals in jets of water hot enough to melt lead.

A young Aboriginal girl leaned over the edge of a sea kayak. The light from the noonday sun penetrated deep into the water and bounced off the chalk drop-off. The girl held a snorkeling mask pressed gently against the roll of the surface water. She could see down clearly, sixty, seventy feet, to where the bubbles from her brother Arnhem's scuba tank danced up through branches of huge gorgon fans and brain coral. Clownfish milled below the dark, muscular body of the young diver. He was searching today down near the end of light.

The girl wished she could talk to Arnhem. *You have been down too long. Too deep. The air in your tank is nearly gone. There are only minutes left to look for the Secret.*

Arnhem saw the kayak above him as a shimmering, blue twig. He knew Maruul would be worried. He had hoped the treasure might be in a cave along the chalk cliff. Or that he would find a slab of pictographs carved into one of the mineral towers. He cleared water from his mask, and kept swimming with the bold, powerful strokes he had learned in the billabong on his tribe's homeland: a pond far away, beyond the mountains, where the water was fresh and his eyes never burned.

He lowered his head, thrust his rubber fins harder, and went deeper. He heard a shrill, mechanical scream.

EEEEEE. EEEE.

He believed that somewhere, nearby, a large motor had started.

Above, the girl had seen Arnhem heading farther down. No, she thought. No! Then she too heard the high-pitched sound. She looked up from the mask. An old, rust-spotted freighter was anchored out beyond the reef. She thought of waving and calling out so anyone aboard would know they were diving in the area. But the ship's deck was deserted.

EEEEEEEEE.

The creature heard the sound, too. It moved its huge tail and pushed water with its immense, powerful pectoral fins. It rose fast up through the hot darkness above the center mound. Its gut shook—contracted—pumped enzymes into its stomach. Through the gnarled sensory lobes on its back, the excited creature crudely understood the sound was its message to feast.

Arnhem found no treasure in the underwater cliff. No mysterious drawings on a chilled, dead tower. Then the shadow, a roll of liquid night, exploded into sight beneath him. At first he was confused. He stared down as the huge specter lightened, grayed in its rush upward toward the light. Arnhem realized that something large, something alive and unthinkable, was swimming straight for him. He started kicking frantically for the surface.

The creature locked on its prey. It saw the boy kicking and could hear his rushed, panicked breathing. A second later, it was close enough to smell him.

Terrified, Arnhem glanced down, saw the mouth of the tremendous fish open into a glowing slab of white teeth the size of daggers. He had been warned about great whites and their jaws that could bite—and slice—three hundred times harder than any animal, sharks that could devour seals, turtles, license plates. But the demon fish he saw now was beyond the crocodile fear of the bush swamps. Beyond the fear of death. Beyond time.

He kicked violently, thrusting himself upward. His sister saw his face twisted by terror. The huge, mutant fish was closing. She reached into the water. She prayed she could grab her brother's hands and pull him up into the sea kayak.

EEEEEEE. EEEE. EEEE.

Jaws snapped on Arnhem's torso like a vise. For a moment, he felt release, as though the wind had been knocked out of him. His arms stretched upward helplessly, his fingers clawing toward the sweet face of his sister. He saw her horror, her hand thrust down toward him. He felt himself shaken violently, then the pain as though a thousand needles were hammered into his stomach. The taste of blood filled his mouth. In his final second alive, he saw a long, red eel bursting out of his waist.

Maruul screamed. She saw Arnhem's intestines and legs fall away from him. A shudder racked her body and she began to choke uncontrollably. It *had* to be a dream, an impossible nightmare! The creature dove to follow the sinking limbs. It snapped at them as the girl saw Arnhem's torso float up to the surface, saw the white flash of spine and the circle of shredded, raw flesh.

The great fish rose again and seized what was left of the corpse. It closed its jaws and plunged down through a red cloud of blood, back toward the blackness of the deep.

Later, when they found the girl, she was shivering in the bottom of the kayak. Her body lay curled tight like a fetus.

She was still screaming.

TWO

THE CALL

The second week of summer break, PC McPhee had the distinct feeling his entire family was going down the tubes. His mother had joined a "For Women Only" club, and his father was obsessed with seeing old Jean-Claude Van Damme movies. Even his grandmother Helen had grown weirder than usual. Gone were family Scrabble nights and going to Giants games. There was no more Pictionary or watching the six-o'clock TV news together. They all floated past each other in the hallways of the McPhee San Francisco home as though they were sealed in Glad wrap.

All PC found himself doing was playing Seven Dirty Dwarves, Magnum Tetris Attack, and Diehard Demon-3, the computer games that had helped him earn his nickname. His real name was Peter Collins McPhee, but no one called him that anymore.

No one.

Lately, on the rare night when his family managed to eat together, everyone got on his case.

"Your uncle Cliff called for you this morning from Cairns, Australia," Grandma Helen told PC. "He wants you to fly down and help him and not be a sloth this summer."

"Why didn't you tell me before?" PC said.

"I just remembered," Grandma Helen said. "I can't tell you anything unless I think of it, you know."

"It's probably just one more of his get-rich schemes," Mrs. McPhee said. "Remember when he had PC fly down to Costa Rica to help him launch an 'international jewelry enterprise'? That turned out to be three women sitting under a banana tree gluing glitter onto the backs of dead beetles."

"Hey," PC said, "at least Uncle Cliff tried something."

"New isn't always good, PC," Mr. McPhee said, and started laughing. "There was that summer he had you come down to sell time-shares in a Yucatán lagoon resort and . . ."

"And it turned out the lagoon was crocodile infested!" Mrs. McPhee said. She giggled.

PC remembered that trip well. He had had terrible dreams about being eaten alive by crocodiles for months after he came back. The nightmares had turned into a deep-seated fear whenever he went near water—but he never told anyone about it.

"All your uncle Cliff's schemes earned a big bagel," Grandma Helen said. "A zero."

"Yeah, but I had fun, and he taught me how to scuba dive, kick box, and dance the rumba." PC pushed a clump of hair out of his eyes and finished chewing a mouthful of roast lamb. "Where's his number?"

Grandma Helen passed the mint jelly and a platter of steaming carrots and broccoli. "I don't know. I wrote it down somewhere, but I think I threw it out with the garbage."

PC groaned.

"Don't worry," Mrs. McPhee said. "He'll call back."

PC had liked Grandma Helen a lot in the beginning when she had come to live with them, but lately she'd started to act like a crazed Mediterranean witch. She'd started snoring, letting out screams in the middle of the night, and sometimes sounding like she was talking in tongues. It had started to freak out PC's friends when they stayed overnight. Grandma Helen's main new shortcoming was that she'd started falling asleep while cooking, and burned pots.

After dinner, Mr. McPhee came to PC's room. "Your mother and I have decided to drive to a Native American casino for the night. She's got a yen to play video poker. I'll sit at a blackjack table."

"Okay," PC said.

His father got his usual accountant's encased-in-plastic look. "You know, I'm doing the books for a Dial-a-Sleep factory. If you don't get to fly down to see your crazy uncle, maybe you'd like a job this summer delivering mattresses."

"Nice."

PC stayed awake long after his parents had left. He watched a rerun of *X-Files*, *Mad Max—Beyond Thunderdome*, and a special on the Discovery Channel about burial rites throughout the world. As a last-ditch attempt to fall asleep, he turned to *Skin Diver* magazine. Seven men and women had written about their most exciting dives. One said his was off Queensland, Australia.

Visible from the moon, the Great Barrier Reef is the world's largest living thing. The monuments of humans are humble before the awesome accomplishment of the tiny polyps that have created the reef—the great mystery fringing the splendid outdoor playground Down Under. . . .

At three A.M., PC woke up to a shocking scream. He thought a Chilean death squad had broken down the front door of the house and that a shrieking woman was being killed. Ribbons of smoke curled toward the light from his TV.

"Grandma Helen!"

PC bolted out of bed. In the hallway, he saw Helen emerging from the black smoke that was pouring out of the kitchen. She looked drunk, waving a big soup pot with its bottom burned out. "Potatoes. I forgot I was boiling potatoes."

He shot by her, checked the kitchen for flames. A chunk of residual green enamel was roasting on a cooling electric burner. He opened a window, snapped a towel up at the screeching smoke alarm on the ceiling, then realized he was barefoot stepping on cooked potatoes. "Ouch! You could have killed us," PC said.

An odd smile crept across Helen's face as she came back into the kitchen. For a moment, her eyes rolled up into the top of her head and she looked like an embarrassed little girl throwing an epileptic fit. Then her eyes rolled back down. PC squirmed under her stare.

"You should go to Australia," she said. "You've had enough of San Francisco. Enough of steep hills and gender benders. Enough of fog. You need to feed koalas and visit termite mounds. Your uncle Cliff said he needs your help with a young girl. An Aboriginal girl. And he wants you to help find a sacred treasure."

"A *sacred treasure*?" PC looked at her long and hard to see if she was making the whole thing up.

"That's what he said."

"Why didn't you tell me that at dinner?"

"I just remembered that part," she said. "And oh, yes—he said it was urgent."

"Are you sure you threw his number out?"

"No, I'm not." Helen began looking through a slew of Day-Glo-green stickies she'd plastered all over the side of the refrigerator. "Oh, here it is," she said, pleased, grabbing one of the stickies. She pressed it into PC's hand.

"Thanks a lot," PC said. He went to the kitchen wall phone and dialed the number on the paper. After several rings, his uncle answered. "I knew you wouldn't let me down, good buddy," Cliff said. "I could really use your help."

"What's up?"

"It's a nuthouse down here."

PC heard the excitement crackling in his uncle's voice. "What?"

"Spooky stuff. Right up your alley," Cliff said. "This time we can have it all, PC! Fortune! Adventure! Fame! Man, it's the chance of a lifetime for us Down Under in Australia. *And your plane leaves at noon!*"

The Qantas 767 jet descended to 12,000 feet before it broke free from clouds above the Coral Sea. PC looked down from his window as the dark blue of the ocean met the string of blue-green islands and shoals that made up the Great Barrier Reef.

He punched some buttons on Ratboy, his laptop. The nickname had popped into his head one day when he was using a mouse. Mouse and Ratboy. Ratboy and mouse. It had made him laugh. GREAT BARRIER REEF, 2,000 kilometers long, off the eastern coast of QUEENSLAND . . .

PC checked a series of travel agency home

pages. Everything that came up gave him an adrenaline rush: *Dive with whale sharks. Feed 200-pound potato cods. Explore shipwrecks.*

"All electronics must be stowed" came over the loudspeaker. PC adjusted his seat to the upright position and got prepared for the landing.

The Cairns airport was crowded with international travelers: women in white slacks and dresses, men in crisp, loud suits. Others were grunge-dressed for the outback. PC's flight was forty minutes early. He washed up, brushed his teeth, and put on a clean T-shirt. He picked up his luggage and made it through customs.

His uncle stood out—tall, tanned, beaming—in the mob of waiting relatives, tour guides, and drivers greeting the plane.

"Hey, buddy," Uncle Cliff said, giving him a hug.

"Hi."

Cliff held him back, looked him over. "You've been working out."

PC grinned. "Yeah. Running. Weights, three times a week. Swimming."

"You're going to need it all." Cliff grabbed PC's large canvas suitcase. "Let's get out of here. I'll catch you up on the way." PC tossed on his favorite cap, black-and-tan camouflage with a Cliff Dwellers patch and Indian stick figures on the front. He carried his backpack as Cliff led the way past the crowded duty-free shop and car rentals out to the short-term parking lot. He stopped at a red convertible, opened the trunk, and tossed in PC's suitcase.

"Nice Mercedes."

"Special lease from Budget." Cliff swung behind the wheel. PC knew Cliff had always needed a flashy car. He was his mother's youngest brother, thirty-eight years old, and still into image. A swimmer's build. Blue jeans and Italian loafers. The only thing wrong was that when Uncle Cliff had $10,000 in a bank, he usually owed somebody else $20,000.

"What's this about an Aboriginal girl and a sacred treasure?" PC asked, as they drove away from the airport.

"It's a long story. Complicated. Maruul—that's the girl's name—will have to tell you about it. She's got partial amnesia now. She was out with her brother diving, looking for the treasure. We think he drowned. Maybe a shark got him. She must have seen it. That's the part she can't remember. We're going to pick her up at the hospital now."

"Then what?" PC asked.

"She wants us to take her back out to the reef. She's stubborn. Also, she's very good-looking and has big eyes that make you want to do things for her. Says she's going to find out what happened to her brother."

Maruul looked up at the striped blue-and-red canopy over the entrance of the hospital. *Whaaack. Whaaack.* It snapped like a heartbeat in the hot wind blowing off Parramatta Park. "Take the straps off," she ordered the nurse. Maruul felt like biting the mean, lanky woman in her starched white uniform and ridiculous matching cap.

Nurse Van Dieman stayed behind the wheelchair, grasping its handles. She had the distinct urge to unbuckle the chair restraints and dump the girl onto the footpath. "You stay put until your ride comes. It's hospital policy for discharges."

Maruul kept watch down Severin Street, hoping to see Cliff. He was late. In the next moment, tears swelled in her eyes. She found herself crying. *Arnhem. What happened to you? Why can't I remember?*

She had eaten the vile breakfast the hospital served. Burned eggs. Fried, hard ham. A seeded roll. She kept going over her life before the last dive. Remembering. Afraid another piece of her mind would click off. She was sixteen and would have graduated from her boarding school. She could have gone on to college. She had hopes of becoming a painter. Or a nurse.

Maybe not a nurse.

Another thought of Arnhem crept into her mind. A memory of her bravest and favorite brother. The elders had coated his body with white clay for his manhood ceremony. They had used the end of a twig, drawn the beautiful, intricate markings of the clan on his skin. The elders had woven bean vines and flowers into bracelets for his arms. They had made him into a living work of art, ready for his ten-day circumcision rite. Maruul remembered seeing Arnhem's proud face—his majestic walk—when he returned from the bush as a full man.

I'll find what happened to you, Arnhem, she promised. I swear it.

THREE

TOWARD THE DREAMING

Cliff slowed the Mercedes as they came into town from the north beaches along The Esplanade, toward Marlin Jetty and Trinity Wharf. PC spotted the Cairns Ramada. Dundee's Restaurant. Huge electric billboards advertised butterfly farms, wildlife sanctuaries, and parasailing.

"The girl and her brother came from a village south of Milingimbi," Cliff said. "We're talking twelve, thirteen hundred kilometers from here."

Cliff looked over, saw PC pulling up a map of Australia on his laptop. "It's west of the Cape York Peninsula in a region called Arnhem Land. Her brother was named after it. He was your age—seventeen. The girl's from the Morga tribe."

PC moved the map grid across Ratboy's screen, past Queensland and the Gulf of Carpentaria. He found Arnhem Land south of the Arafura Sea.

"Why did they come to the reef?" PC asked.

"They were chosen as *arukas.* That translates

from her tribe's language as 'seekers.' The elders of her village took her out of boarding school. She's an *aruka* because she's smart and speaks English. Her brother was the best swimmer. He had what they call 'the water dreaming.' Maruul will tell you about their religion. They've got lots of myths and folklore."

Cliff made a sharp turn by the railway station and onto Bunda Street.

"How did Maruul and Arnhem find you?" PC wanted to know.

"An Aboriginal man owns a dive shop near Cape Tribulation. He put them onto me. I had just bought a boat and diving equipment. They offered to work as crew in exchange for private dive time."

"They wanted to look for the treasure?"

"Right. I leased a mooring platform on the reef south of Half Moon Island. The Reef's hot now. Tourists pay five, ten thousand dollars for a charter-dive package."

"You're *kidding*."

"I'm hooking up with hotels. Another month or so and I'll have everything in place to be a first-class tourist diving operation. Eventually, I want to offer black marlin fishing. And swim with whale sharks. Everything."

PC's cap began to lift in the wind. He swung the visor around backward. "Exactly what is the sacred treasure?"

"Nobody knows. The girl's tribe believes in a legend that some kind of fortune on the outer reef belongs to them. The tribe left it there a long time ago when they moved west. Now that the village is in trouble, Maruul and Arnhem were sent to bring a part of the treasure back. She says the village needs to buy food and hire lawyers."

"Why lawyers?"

"A lot of big business guys and sleazy politicos are trying to steal the Morgas' land. Maruul says most of Australia's turned into a big pie, and everyone wants a piece of it. All kinds of crooks are coming out of the woodwork to cheat Aboriginal people out of their farmland and mining rights. One cartel destroyed the Morgas' hunting by burning all the land around the village. The tribe needs to fight them in court. Maruul says children are starving. Her village's holy man—their shaman—has disappeared. They think he's been kidnapped, probably killed, by some company's henchmen."

"Why didn't the Morgas take the treasure with them when they left a long time ago?"

"See, now, that's a big thing with Aboriginal people," Cliff said, swerving the car left to avoid hitting a mud-covered sow and her piglets. The sow squealed and turned onto the shoulder of the road. "They have this spiritual belief: *Take from the land and oceans only that which you need, and no more.*"

"Sounds like they think of their treasure like a bank account," PC said.

"Right," Cliff agreed. "From everything Maruul tells me about them, they're really good people. She said we can have a share of the treasure if we can help find it—but I wanted to help them anyway."

Nurse Van Dieman released the wheelchair bindings the moment Cliff pulled the Mercedes up to the hospital entrance. Maruul stumbled woozily out of the chair into Cliff's arms. "Don't tip her," she mumbled, as Cliff helped her into the backseat of the car. "She's a creep."

Cliff took Maruul's small, beat-up, blue-metal suitcase and put it in the trunk. PC grabbed her army-surplus knapsack and passed it back to her.

"I'm PC," he told her.

Maruul looked at him, then at the open glowing screen of the laptop.

"This is Ratboy," PC said, smiling.

She looked worn out and hassled, but she was as beautiful as Cliff had said she was. She'd woven her night-black hair into a cluster of long, thin braids, each one with an amber bead at the end of it. He settled back into the front passenger seat as Cliff slid behind the wheel.

"The Coast Guard radioed the bush station that your brother is missing," Cliff told Maruul. "There'll be a message waiting for your dad whenever he comes in. You still want to head back up to the reef?"

"Yes." Maruul closed her eyes. Her thoughts were spinning and she felt dizzy. She decided to think of her family. She could imagine her father under a tall eucalyptus tree with his paintbrushes and bench. His eyes would be strained as he hunched over a wood-bark painting. She thought of her caring and loving twenty-seven mothers and thirty-two younger brothers and sisters back in her village. She thought of their hunger and the evil men burning the land around her village. Their greed and their hatred of the Aboriginal people. She thought of many things she would never be able to explain completely to the kind white man called Cliff. Or the boy.

PC.

The strange-named boy who had come from the USA.

On the drive north, PC saw men and children fishing from rocky groines and jetties. Women dug for shellfish. There was a series of bridges that carried them over tidal waterways and lush banks covered with mangroves and twisting aerial roots. For a while he watched Maruul sleeping in the backseat.

They arrived at Cape Tribulation at sunset. Cliff left his car parked at a private marina edging the south of the bay. He woke up Maruul. She and PC helped him carry the gear down to his boat slip.

"This is it," Cliff said, boarding the *Sea Quest*, a thirty-six-foot dive skiff. He pulled the canvas off the main bay. It was lined on both sides with air tanks and diving equipment. "All aboard." He threw open a cowling to check the oil and gas feeds to the inboard motor.

"It looks fast," PC said.

"It is." Cliff started the engine. "Get the ties. I want us out at the mooring before dark."

PC threw off the bow rope, tossed it onto the decking. Maruul untied the stern. They jumped aboard. Cliff shifted into forward, then inched the throttle ahead. The boat cruised out into the mouth of the channel. After they were past the last of the coastal buoys, Cliff opened the throttle wide.

The propellers roared, dug in, and lifted the bow above the horizon. The hull slapped noisily against the waves until the boat broke from the coast and into the main lagoon. Behind them, the beach was a white crescent at the foot of mountains of rain forest rising up to touch the clouds.

Maruul and PC sat on the front deck, wind crashing into their faces. The small amber beads from her braids danced and clicked against each other. A dozen kilometers from the coast, the Great Barrier Reef lay beneath shallow waters like the body of a sleeping giant. PC saw the vast coral shoals and strips of patch rock that made up the reef. Finally, the skiff neared the outer edge where the reef met an infinity of dark-blue sea.

"There it is!" Cliff shouted.

PC saw the mooring platform and its stark white canvas fluttering in the breeze. Maruul looked toward the setting sun as Cliff docked the skiff next to the kayak. At the sight of the kayak, she remembered Arnhem and began to tremble.

The sky was afire with crimson and gold as Cliff finished cooking steaks in the skiff's galley. Maruul had managed to chop a lettuce-and-kiwi-fruit salad. PC set the table for them in the cabana.

"Whose minisub?" PC called out as he finished checking the platform. He had found a two-person open submersible hanging from a pair of launch arms.

"I bought it secondhand," Cliff said, bringing the platter of meat and vegetables to the table. "You're nobody in this business unless you offer tourists a submersible. You get wet, but it holds two. A battery powers a turbine with a lot more kick than the one we used off Mexico."

PC noticed the antishark bars curving over

the sub's cockpit. He remembered the minisub in Cancún. They had gone there to be part of a team photographing predatory sharks. That submersible had had a fully caged cockpit. PC had stayed in it, knowing he was safe. Cliff had taken chances, as usual, swimming out with the sharks. He wanted to show the dive master he was braver.

Bolder.

It was a trait of his uncle's that PC knew could be dangerous.

During dinner, PC caught Maruul staring at him. "Did you and Arnhem think about using the submersible?" he asked her.

"Yes," she said. "But Arnhem thought we should explore with the kayak first—to make certain we were in the right area."

"Were you?" PC asked.

"Yes," Maruul said.

"How could you know?"

"Show PC the painting," Cliff said to Maruul. She got up from the table and opened her neon-blue metal suitcase. A photo of Maruul with a boy was taped on the inside lid.

"Is this your brother?" PC asked.

Maruul nodded. PC turned the case toward a

lamp. Arnhem's dark, handsome face stared out from the photo. He had a full, open smile. A single silver earring in the shape of a snake hung from his right ear.

"Arnhem was given the silver earring at his manhood ceremony," Maruul said. "A silver earring is a very great honor in the Morga tribe."

She reached in and took out a flat rectangle wrapped in an old, crudely woven blanket. She carried it to the table. Cliff brought an extra Coleman lamp from the skiff and turned it on.

Maruul unwrapped a long piece of painted bark. The images of an ocher sun, violent blue water, and ghostly figures were striking. "Even our maps are paintings. Dreams. Visions from our minds," Maruul said. "It is the same style in which my father was taught to paint, and he, in turn, taught me." She pointed to a distinctive gold form at the top of the map. "We know from this land shape that this is Half Moon Island."

Cliff said, "It's just north of here. Whoever made the map didn't know distances, but they picked solid markers."

PC recognized the serpentlike shape of the reef between the hundreds of green lagoons and midnight-blue ocean in the painting. "But how could anyone know exactly where to look for the treasure?"

"We speak and paint our legends and stories in pictures and symbols. But there's a song-riddle my village's elders have passed down through the years. It was taught to me in the language of my people. I've tried my best to put it into words a non-Aboriginal person could understand."

She began to sing in a delicate, haunting soprano voice:

> *"Night will bring the mystery.*
> *Moonlight points the way.*
> *Sunset hides beneath the sea,*
> *But dawn the beast will slay."*

"What does it mean?" PC asked.

Maruul pointed to four tiny silver baby hands painted so they appeared to be clutching the bottom of the map. "Arnhem figured out the 'points the way' part," Maruul said. "The silver baby hands. They each have a finger pointing." Maruul pulled out a sheet of tracing paper and placed it on top of the map. She took a ruler, extended straight pencil lines up from each of the pointing fingers. They all intersected at one point on the bark.

"That's where we are now," Cliff said. "At least, we're very near it."

"Arnhem and I went out in the kayak," Maruul said, her voice growing quiet and frightened. "I don't know if I can remember anything more. . . ."

"You were on the kayak looking for the treasure," Cliff said.

"Yes."

Maruul felt a pain in her head. She closed her eyes and covered her face with her hands. She knew she had to try to remember. "Arnhem wanted to do a final deep dive alone. That's all I see . . . my brother swimming deeper. . . ."

Cliff looked to PC.

"You said your father taught you to paint. That means you can draw, right, Maruul?" PC asked.

"Yes."

She looked up and watched PC get his laptop and bring it to the table. He turned it on. "Let's try something." He brought up an art-board program, plugged in the stylus, and placed it in Maruul's hand. "Draw."

"I don't understand."

"Draw what you saw from the boat. What you saw in the water," PC said. "Let your mind drift. Just do it. Don't think about it."

Maruul lifted the stylus to the glowing screen. A thin black line appeared. She wiggled the stylus, then pressed harder, and the line expanded into wider, brushlike strokes. "I remember the kayak," she said. "I can see Arnhem down deep. Alone. His mask." She made zigzag lines, like a heartbeat on an oscilloscope.

"What else do you see?" PC asked.

"There is something . . . down deep," Maruul said. "Something coming up . . . toward Arnhem . . . and *me*. . . ."

"Draw it," PC said.

"I can't."

"Try."

Maruul squirmed in her seat. Slowly, she made a form take shape on the screen. At first, PC thought it was a type of shark. But it was more primitive. A swollen thing with streamers hanging from it. Lumps on its back.

Maruul's arm began to shake as she moved her hand faster. She drew huge, ghastly eyes on the fish. Hornlike structures thrust out from its brow. She began to gasp, and tears filled her eyes. She gave the creature a mouth—a huge mouth with daggerlike teeth.

A high-pitched wail rose from Maruul's mouth, its pitch growing higher and higher.

Until it became a scream.

For a long while the three of them stared at the terrifying sketch on the computer screen. Cliff put his arm around Maruul's shoulders. PC assured her the creature wasn't real.

"Cliff and I will dive wherever you want," PC said. "A great white may have gotten Arnhem, but what you've drawn is from a bad dream. It doesn't exist."

"He's right," Cliff said.

"I'm not sure," she said, dropping her head into her hands again. "I'm not sure at all."

PC stayed up long after his uncle and Maruul had gone to their bunks on the skiff. He wanted to think and stretched out on a cot in the cabana. He went over the bark painting with a fine-tooth comb and typed the song-riddle onto Ratboy. He ran each of the nouns through the computer's thesaurus. Nothing struck him as having a trick meaning, and a lot could have been lost in translation. He concentrated on the second line of the riddle: "Moonlight points the way." If Arnhem was right about the baby hands pointing the way, then there had to be a connection between "moonlight" and the baby hands. If he could find out what that was, he'd have a handle on the rest of the riddle.

He turned off the Coleman. The grisly image Maruul had drawn still haunted him. And made him think about his greatest fear. The fear he never told to anyone. A fear that was always in the back of his head whenever he went on a dive.

The fear of being eaten alive.

Finally, after two A.M., jet lag socked into him and he fell asleep.

FOUR

SECOND BLOOD

Cliff was up early. He moved the mini-sub into tow position behind the skiff and checked the *Sea Quest*'s masks, wet suits, and diving fins. He had invested in two dozen 420-denier nylon dive vests resistant to punctures, with tank mounts and Velcro closures. He cleaned and calibrated three of the Spectrum XP regulators.

PC groaned as Maruul tied open the cabana flaps to let the morning sun hit him in the face.

"Wake up, lazy," she called out. "Skipper's ready."

PC got up and grabbed a cup of coffee in the skiff's galley. He put on a wet suit and came up on deck as they were cruising south along the outer edge of the reef. Maruul watched off the starboard.

"You and Arnhem came this way in the kayak?" PC asked.

"Yes," Maruul said. She coughed as she felt a painful mixture of sadness and fear grip her throat. "I remember Arnhem was sure we were at the point marked on the map. It looks different today. We came at high tide. All the reef was underwater."

PC shielded his eyes from the glare of the sun. The water was crystal green. Sections of the reef protruded above water, some volcanic rock and coral ledges rising as much as six, seven feet. The ocean waves rolled gently up onto the reef, then broke into small white crests that blended with the tidal pools and lagoons.

A black freighter was anchored off the reef in an area of the sea that was darker, rougher. "What's that boat doing there?" PC asked, pointing ahead. It had *Anemone* stenciled on its bow in big white letters.

Maruul, her brow wrinkled, looked toward the freighter. "I remember it was nearby when Arnhem decided to dive."

"It flies a Malaysian flag," Cliff said. "I checked it out before leasing the platform. Belongs to some big corporation. It's been converted into a floating research lab."

"A lab?" PC said.

"That's what the Coast Guard told me. There are underwater volcanic vents in the ocean here. Underwater mineral towers. The Australian government gave the *Anemone* permission to test for chemicals. Temperatures. That sort of thing."

A pained expression crept onto Maruul's face. "There was a sound of a motor coming from the freighter. Something different from a regular ship's engine. It made an earsplitting noise while Arnhem was diving. It was strange, because the deck was deserted."

"It could have been the sound of an underwater drill," PC said. "They're probably drilling."

"They're not supposed to," his uncle said.

A recess with shining ledges had been eroded into the reef for a hundred yards along the surface. One turquoise-and-pink shelf jutted out ten or twenty feet before a blazing white underwater cliff dropped into an abyss. PC noticed Maruul's body stiffening. "You recognize something?"

"This is definitely where Arnhem and I were in the kayak. I remember the whiteness."

"A chalk wall," Cliff said. He slowed the boat to a crawl. "A mixture of coral, dolomite, and zinc oxides from the sea vents."

Maruul looked toward the freighter, then

back down to the underwater cliff. "Arnhem thought the treasure would be here."

"This is right according to the map," Cliff said. He maneuvered the skiff until it floated above a strip of volcanic rock, then dropped anchor. "We have to be careful. Some of this coral can cut a dive suit to pieces. You and Maruul explore the cliff in the sub. I'll check the ledges, then catch up."

"There might be a marker only I would recognize," Maruul said. "A sign of my village."

PC nodded. "She's right. You two take the submersible."

"No. The ledges are too shallow. Waves will crash the sub." Cliff stepped down to the stern swim platform and readied the sub for boarding. "You take it alone," he told PC. "We'll meet on the cliff face."

PC put on a pair of rubber tennis shoes. He slipped into the sleek fiberglass cockpit of the sub and closed the steel shark bars over him. "Don't dive much deeper than a hundred feet or so," his uncle said. "The nearest decompression chamber's forty minutes away at the Cape."

PC fit snugly in the forward bucket seat, his

legs stretched out in front of him. Cliff passed
him his fins to store in a netted side compartment. "In case you want to leave the sub
and explore. Take this, too." He handed over
a two-and-a-half-foot black stick with a thick-
ened tip.

"A bang stick?" PC asked.

"Yes. Explosive head like the ones we trained
with off Cancún. This one'll handle a mako. No
bullet. Kills by impact."

PC secured the weapon and started the sub's
motor. The rotors whirled powerfully, silently,
like a fan. He felt uneasy about leaving Maruul
with Cliff. He might show off as he had in
Mexico. Take chances. "You guys be careful," he
called.

Maruul gave a small wave. "You, too."

PC set his mask and breather in place. He
nudged the throttle forward and taxied, circling
at the surface until Maruul and Cliff had their
masks and fins in place. They rechecked the regulators and air tanks, then dropped backward
off the swim platform. PC trailed them as they
went under and swam for the shallows of the
long, glistening ledge.

• • •

After a few minutes, PC got the feel for the mini-sub and was able to compensate for the strong undercurrent near the reef. He stayed thirty feet off the face of the chalk cliff until he was solid on the controls. A fissure in the whiteness of the wall made him turn, travel slowly to explore its cavity.

At the mouth of the fissure, a coral tower rose from the ocean floor. As PC circled it, a harmless, small Port Jackson shark passed him, looking for food. A cloud of butterfly fish and purple basslets swarmed into the open water. There were shining angelfish. Huge, gracefully diving green sea turtles. A brilliantly yellow rabbitfish. Mushroom coral, sea fans, and black, spiny sea urchins were clustered in startling colonies.

If he had a treasure, PC thought, he would hide it in this beautiful place.

EEEEEEE. EEEE.

Maruul heard the high-pitched sound and recognized it at once. She signaled to Cliff that she was swimming to one of the shallow ledges. When she reached it, she managed to stand in her fins and lift her head up into the air. She slid off her mask and breathed deeply. Cliff joined her.

"That's the sound I heard before," Maruul said. She felt suddenly sick to her stomach.

Cliff looked out beyond the anchored skiff to the distant freighter. "It's drilling, all right."

Her mind still hadn't retrieved all of her last day with Arnhem. The bright sunlight. Whiteness. The kayak. She had been convinced that the monstrosity she'd drawn on the computer screen was fiction, a bad dream from a dark, cryptic corner of her brain—but her mind was still playing tricks. She had felt confident a minute before, swimming along the edge of the reef, excited that at any moment she might find the treasure.

"Maybe we should get out of the water," she said.

"Hey, we've checked almost the whole ledge," Cliff said. "We might as well finish the rest of it; then you can go with PC in the sub."

Maruul's thoughts turned to sharks. If there was no monster, there might well be a great white. Even in her village she'd heard people could be attacked by sharks in shallow water. An Aboriginal woman had been taken by her ankles—devoured in front of children and tourists at a beach near her boarding school.

She tried to push her fears away.

"I'll swim in front," Cliff offered.

"Okay," Maruul said.

Cliff dove, his flippers kicking above the water, then sinking slowly. She followed him under and continued to scan the ledge. But the bad feeling came again.

GET OUT OF THE WATER.

An inner voice echoed in her mind.

GET OUT.

PC, too, had heard the high-pitched sound. It *was* like a drill, he thought. He was certain the sound was coming from the freighter. By now, the maneuvering of the submersible had become automatic. He followed a school of batfish deeper into the winding passageway of the fissure. A glittering ribbon, a striation running down the center of a rock wall, caught his eye. The band started two feet from the surface, then plunged down a hundred feet into blackness. The undercurrent was gentle here. He brought the sub in closer.

The shining strip looked like silver. He

loosened a buckle on his suit and used it as a tool. The metal was malleable, soft enough to shave. He slid the sample into a pouch in his diving vest, then reached back to the shining strip.

Suddenly, the dark, ugly head of a fat eel flew out from a hole in the rock wall. Its long, slimy body rippled like a flag as it sank its needlelike teeth into the arm of his wet suit.

YOW!

PC's startled cry released a rush of bubbles. His eyes were wide behind his mask.

A second ghastly head shot out from the hole and locked onto his wrist. He yanked his arm back, but the eels held on like bulldogs. Their bodies thrashed, churned against him inside the cockpit.

PC had never seen a moray eel attack divers unless they'd accidentally prodded it in its den. The eels shook their bodies savagely, powerfully, each determined to tear off a piece of his flesh. The sub spun out of control and careened toward the mouth of the fissure.

PC desperately tried to rub the eels off, crush them against the cage bars. They held on. And on. Until a massive, impossible shadow rose like a mountain in front of the sub.

"Oh, God."

Quickly, the eels let go and raced for safety back into the crevice. PC gasped as he watched the new arrival—a huge, dark form—drift closer toward him. The eels were merely a prelude, he realized, to a horror beyond his imagination. He began to tremble.

A pair of large, yellowing eyes floated closer to him. He saw the giant ganglia rising out of the brow. The fins of the monstrosity churned the water, tilting the sub. The creature shook spastically, furiously, and its jaws opened to reveal its megamouth of teeth. You're real, PC thought, aghast. You're *real*.

PC was paralyzed for a moment by the sight of the horror, then grabbed the controls and turned the sub sharply farther back into the fissure. The creature followed, crashing violently into the narrowing sides of the passageway. Its mouth closed, then opened again to gnash insanely at the chalk walls.

EEEEEEEE. EEEE.

The sound from the freighter was piercing now. PC thought the sound seemed to affect the fish, to infuriate it even more. The water where it snapped and thrashed was a boiling cauldron, its force pushing the sub deeper into the crevice. The frenzied creature was too huge to follow.

But Cliff and Maruul . . . he had to warn them.

He released a blast of compressed air. The sub rose fast.

Too fast.

It kept slamming against the sides of the crevice until it burst from the surface. PC swung open the cockpit cage, threw off his mask and tank, and scrambled out onto a strip of exposed reef. His tennis shoes gripped the sharp, cutting coral as he ran. He saw Cliff and Maruul standing waist deep on a ledge. A mammoth shadow moved toward them from the open water. The creature had found them.

PC's shout split the air:

"GET OUT! GET OUT!"

They turned to see PC yelling, looked out to where he was pointing. They saw the darkness heading for them.

The sight cracked the last wall of memory in Maruul's mind. She remembered Arnhem kicking madly for the surface. Arnhem reaching for her hand. The full nightmare. She backed toward the reef wall.

Cliff followed her. They threw off their flippers and tanks—and tried to climb. The wall was too steep, too slippery.

Deep gaps in the reef separated PC from them. He turned and raced back to the sub. No time for mask or tank. He slammed the cage bars closed over the cockpit and raced the sub along the surface.

Cliff cupped his hands and tried to boost Maruul out of the water.

"I CAN'T," she cried. "I CAN'T."

The creature was there. Cliff turned to face it. He kept Maruul behind him, hoping the water was too shallow for the fish to strike. The creature's head rose from the surface, its ganglia hanging like snakes. Cliff threw one of the air tanks, then the other. Both struck the fish. It stopped swimming, confused.

Maruul screamed at the fish.

"GO AWAY! GO!"

The creature propelled itself forward like an orca after seals. PC held the throttle open as he raced through the waves. Each second was an infinity as he turned sharply, hurtling toward the ledge. He thought he knew what was going to happen. He wanted to shout to Cliff and

Maruul, tell them he was going to ram the horror—but it was too late. Cliff began to swim along the side of the reef, trying to draw the monster after him.

The fish hesitated, then thrashed until it was at Cliff's side. For a moment it seemed as if it had overshot him, but at the last second it made a lightning grab and dragged him under.

"No!" PC yelled. He revved the motor of the sub, rocking forward so the propeller screamed for a moment in air. He hoped the racket would frighten the fish into letting go of its prey.

He had to get Maruul.

He brought the submersible to her side, threw open the shark bars. She slid into the cockpit, shouting.

"WHERE IS HE? WHERE IS CLIFF?"

Suddenly, they saw the top half of him emerge from the sea. His lips moved, but no sound came out. Maruul and PC didn't understand what was happening.

Then the water below him churned—and they knew.

The creature pulled Cliff back under. PC remembered the bang stick, grabbed it, and clutched it like a sword.

The creature rose again.

Maruul sobbed.

"DON'T LOOK," PC shouted.

Cliff's limp body was impaled on the creature's teeth, its massive jaws shaking him.

The sound of cracking bone.

He saw Cliff's rib cage ripped wide—saw his uncle's lungs and bleeding stomach. With a final bite, jaws closed on Cliff's skull. His face twisted, seeming for a moment an apocalypse reflected from a fun-house mirror—then burst into blood, brains, and bits of bone. The fish tossed its mutilated prey in a red tide, rolling, bubbling, seething. Finally, the creature swallowed Cliff into oblivion.

PC cried out, his heart pounding in his chest. He turned the sub toward a cut in the reef. The sub's power ebbed.

EEEEEE!

Maruul looked up.

"PC. It's coming again," she said.

He saw the monstrous darkness returning.

"Come on, come on," he urged, talking to it as if the thing could understand. The huge fish broke the surface, its jaws crashing down, grinding—then opening again. The bars of the cockpit bent, twisted. PC rose high in his seat, fast, lunging with the bang stick.

Up.

Up.

The explosion happened high in the creature's mouth. There was a flash of fire. Deformed, burned cartilage and skin. It was enough for the fish to stop, to fall away and sink.

PC and Maruul made it to a strip of the dry reef. They tumbled out of the sub and collapsed. The sounds from the dark, deserted freighter had halted. PC fought tears as he lifted the batteries out of the sub and left them to bake in the hot sun. It would bring back a charge.

It had to.

Cliff's dive mask and one of the air tanks rolled in the currents on a reef. Their metal trim flashed as the ocean washed gently over them, touched the reef, and retreated.

There had been three divers.

Now there were two.

The reality rushed in on PC. He knew what they would have to do. He thought of his uncle. Alone. Cliff in a chilling, strange darkness. He began a silent prayer.

Fly, Uncle Cliff.

Go.

Be in a Heaven somewhere.

A Paradise.

Let there be a God and angels and saints.

FIVE

THE MEETING

PC waited until the tide had begun to creep over the last dry ledge before he replaced the battery in the half-mangled sub. No aircraft had flown over. No fishing boats passed by. No one had come to rescue them.

"It—the thing—could be waiting for us," Maruul said.

"We have no choice."

The voltage of the battery had rebounded in the sun, kicking out enough power to get them to the skiff. There had been no terrible dark shadow. No sounds from the *Anemone*. Nothing. PC pulled up anchor and started the engine. The skiff raced north back along the outer reef. He couldn't think straight. They'd have to report everything to the Australian Coast Guard. He'd have to call his mother and father and tell them what had happened to Cliff.

Fear and a terrible sorrow began to consume Maruul. She was damp and hungry. She saw the channel to the main lagoon. She pointed, forced herself to speak. "There's a Coast Guard base near Cape Tribulation," she said.

PC turned the skiff and followed the buoys toward the mainland.

"Why would the spirits make something terrible like that?" Maruul asked. "How could they create such a monster, a thing that can't have any reason for being?"

PC tightened the cables to the battery. "I used to lie awake a lot of nights wondering the same thing about dinosaurs—and imagining God sitting around thinking up all the most terrible killing machines that have ever lived. Raptors and T. rexes with mouths and teeth meant to murder every living thing around them. Lizards with horns and serrated fangs and razor claws. Why did he make great whites and crocodiles and blood-sucking bats? What kind of God is he?"

"I don't know," Maruul said, her eyes filled with tears.

"Every time I go into the water, I think I'm going to be eaten alive by something treacherous, but I go anyway. I force myself to remember all the good things God made on this earth.

I think we've all got to fight the mistakes God made. The treachery and murdering and devouring. I try to believe that all the horror on this planet is caused by a devil. Demons. Not God."

"What were the sounds from the freighter?" Maruul asked. "It was the same with Arnhem. The shrieking from the *Anemone*. Nobody on deck. Just the sounds."

"There's something really weird about that freighter. There had to be somebody aboard. Somebody must have seen what was happening to us," PC said. "And why are they drilling?"

"They probably paid off some politician, like everyone else does in this country."

"Will anyone come for you? Your father?"

"Not for a while." Maruul thought of her village and couldn't find words. Arnhem was gone. She had failed her father and family, the elders and her village.

Arukas. She and Arnhem were supposed to be the great *arukas.* "What's going to happen to my people? There is dysentery. Children's bellies are sore, swollen with disease. The shaman, our village holy man . . ."

"Cliff told me he was kidnapped," PC said.

She looked away, then found her voice again.

"A few days after he was first missing, a child brought a basket to the village. A girl. Six or seven years old. There was blood on her hands. She said a white man had given her the basket. In it was a still-warm human heart."

It was an hour before they found the approach to the Cape Tribulation marina. PC slowed the boat through the NO WAKE zone, guided it to its berth. He'd had a chance to think ahead. "If we report Cliff's death to the Coast Guard now, they'll take whatever he owns. Confiscate it. The skiff. Diving equipment. His gear at the mooring platform. They could do anything. Sell his boat at some rigged auction. The harbor police in Cancún cheated Cliff out of everything he owned."

"And they'll put you on the next plane back to San Francisco," Maruul said.

"You got it." PC jumped onto the dock to tie the bowline.

"We have to talk to Wally W.," Maruul said.

"Wally *who*?"

"A friend. An Aboriginal man who left my village many years ago. Wally Wallygong. He's old now, but the elders told me I can trust

him. His nephew owns the dive shop that out-
fitted Cliff's skiff and mooring platform." She
swung open a storage compartment under the
rear bench on the skiff. "We have to tell him
everything," she said, lifting out her blue-metal
suitcase.

Maruul led the way down the dock to a cluster
of stores and thatched-roof huts. Beyond,
in a clearing, was the Cape Dive Shop—walls
of rainbow-painted concrete block fractured
by jalousied windows. A BACK AT 3 sign hung
on the front door.

"Wally lives around back," Maruul said.

A bank of smoke from a massive junked
ship's boiler socked into them. The top had
been cut, riveted, and hinged to make a lid. PC
choked, kept clear of the smells and fumes. He
rubbed at his eyes and glimpsed a ramshackle
bungalow with an old black man sitting on the
front porch.

"Hello," Wally Wallygong called out. He was
skinny, naked except for tight black corduroy
shorts. An explosion of gray hair and a galloping
beard framed scars on his nose, badges from his
younger life in the bush and on a cattle ranch.

He smiled, leaped up, and gave Maruul a big hug. "Just in time for barbecue, eh. You like yams? Fish, black snake, and lizard?"

"This is my friend—PC," Maruul said.

Wally grabbed PC's hand and pumped it like he was drawing water up from a well.

"Something's happened, eh. . . ." Wally caught the fear in Maruul's eyes. "In that case, I fix you plates of crispy bushtucker. Diet Cokes. You tell me your story, eh," Wally said. He swung open the top of the fiery boiler. PC looked in at the racks of sizzling tubers and charred four-legged carcasses.

"Yams and a Coke for me," PC said.

As they ate, Maruul told Wally about Cliff. The creature. The freighter. The treasure. She showed him the map. Told him the riddle.

He knew about Arnhem. "Sailors, Coast Guard white men stop at dive shop and want barbecue," Wally said. "Can't keep mouths shut. They chatter like chookie chicken birds, eh." He watched them eat as they related their story. When they finished, Wally sat cross-legged in front of them.

"Now it is my turn to talk," Wally said. "Cliff. Arnhem. No need to worry about them.

Marrawuti, the sea eagle, has taken their spirits. Marrawuti circles in the skies, sees all who fade beneath the ocean. He lifts them up. Takes them where they must go, eh."

"We didn't come to you for stories about Marrawuti, the sea eagle," Maruul said.

"I forgot you are modern Aboriginal woman," Wally said. "Forgive me. I know the reef where you lost Cliff and Arnhem. My nephew and I did many dives there. Took many fish. The place of the chalk cliff and the anger of the volcano, eh. It is known as a place of danger and death. There are many creatures like the one you have seen. Demons that live nowhere else. Sailors—Javanese and Borneo men—from the *Anemone* freighter are frightened. They say white men on the ship do terrible experiments. They find small, hairy arms and hands of monkeys floating in water. Other dead animals. Freighter do evil, blood ceremonies."

"I think they know about the treasure," PC said. "It's no coincidence they're drilling out there."

Blood rushed to Maruul's face. "But how could they know? It is sacred and secret to my village."

"Sailors say there is someone from your clan aboard," Wally explained. "A Morga who knows your map and secret ceremonies better than you do."

"That can't be," Maruul said. "Who?"

"You told me the village shaman was missing—about the child bringing you his heart in a basket," Wally said. "When I was living in the village, I never believed in that shaman. I think he had a screw loose."

"Are you saying he could have told someone about the treasure?" PC asked.

"All I'm saying is that he was a faker. He always did a trick with dead dogs. When the young men in the village ever didn't want to do what he told them to, he would find a dead dog. He'd say the dog died of evil and perform a ritual, eh. It was a scary ceremony. He would dance around with fire torches and rub his lips over the body of the dead dog. Suddenly his lips would stop over one part, and he'd take a bite out of the dog. He'd say he had the evil spirit in his mouth and he'd start screaming and shaking and scaring everyone. Then he'd spit the mouthful out into his hand, and we'd see some kind of a lump. He'd jump up and down yelling, 'It's the evil spirit. It's the evil spirit!' He'd run to a hole in the ground, throw the thing in, and bury it."

"How did you know for sure he was a faker?" PC asked.

"Because a friend and I used to dig up all the 'evil spirits' he spit in the ground. It was always an old tooth or piece of broken crockery or some other kind of junk."

"What about the heart in the box?" Maruul wanted to know.

Wally laughed. "I think that shaman would have cut out his mother's heart if he needed it."

"Well, whoever it is, we have to tell somebody who'll stop them," PC said.

Wally looked to PC. "We believe in many spirits. Earth, the mother. Stone and Kangaroo. Lightning man. Owl man. The honey-eater bird whose cry is the spirit of a woman calling out for her lover."

"Wally," Maruul said, interrupting, "my village needs money. We have to find the treasure, if there is one. We don't want to be cheated anymore. We're not going to sit around waiting for old spirits to help us. We're being robbed and threatened and wiped out. We're going to fight the corporate swindlers! We're going to fight them! The Aboriginal lands are being stolen from us!"

Wally went silent. He stared at Maruul as though really seeing her for the first time. "They are stealing your heritage, too, eh," he finally said.

Maruul felt hopelessness crowding in on her again. The fire in her eyes disappeared and was replaced by fear. "What can we do?" she asked softly.

Wally was silent again for a long while. Finally, he spoke.

"You must go back to the reef," he said. "This time with the best guide between Cooktown and Cairns. A guide who, like Arnhem, has the water dreaming. He knows the secrets of the sharks and devilfish, eh. He'll lead you. Make you find the Morga treasure, for small commission. He'll protect you from screaming freighters."

Wally Wallygong stood up and disappeared into the shack. When he came back, he carried a mask and fins. "I am excellent guide. I will go with you," he said. He took a pair of blackened steel tongs, shoved them deep into the hot coals of the barbecue pit, and extracted a steaming, oval-shaped clump. "We take to-night's savory dinner with us. We enjoy on mooring platform out at reef," Wally said. "Nice roasted turtle."

"How old is he?" PC whispered to Maruul, as Wally Wallygong went to slip a note under the door of the dive shop.

"Seventy-four or seventy-nine," Maruul said. "He doesn't know. Old Aboriginal men don't keep track of those things."

They had watched Wally Wallygong scribble on a piece of stained, ripped paper.

Dear Nephew,

I have gone fishing for few days. Call Budget Rent-a-Car. Tell to pick up Cliff's Mercedes. He not need. You and grandchildren eat all delicious barbecue bushtucker.

Wally set the pace heading down the dock for the skiff. PC and Maruul ran after him. Soon they had boarded and PC had the throttle of the boat wide open. Maruul shivered from the wind as the sun began to sink behind the mountains of the rain forest. Wally Wallygong placed a blanket around her shoulders. He sat on the foredeck and sang out loud over the roar of the skiff's engine:

> *"Yea, though I walk through*
> *the Valley of Death,*
> *I shall fear no evil,*
> *la la—*
> *for I am Wally Wallygong,*
> *the meanest kangaroo in the navy,*
> *la la . . ."*

His eyes rolled, shone out from under his gray, crinkled hair. He lifted his arms high as though embracing everything. The lagoon. The sunset. Maruul and PC.

PC decided to test Wally. "What do you think of the riddle?"

"I am good at riddles," the old man said. He turned to Maruul. "Sing it again." She sang softly into his ear:

> *"Night will bring the mystery.*
> *Moonlight points the way.*
> *Sunset hides beneath the sea,*
> *But dawn the beast will slay."*

"I put it on Ratboy," PC said. "Checked synonyms. The baby hands on the map show location, but we haven't been able to catch the connection between night, moonlight, sunset, and dawn."

"Have you tried *colors*?" Wally shot at them. "Moonlight is silver. Map has silver hands. Night is black. Black Aboriginal person must bring mystery map. Is easy riddle."

"What about *sunset*?" PC asked.

"Color of the fortune. Could be red garnets. Blue diamonds. Silver."

"Take the wheel," PC told Maruul. She slid into the pilot seat. He got his dive vest, opened the Velcro pocket. He took out the thin strip of metal he had scraped from the reef. "What do you think of this? Is it silver?"

Wally took the shard, turned it over in his palm. He bit on it, looked to see his deep teeth marks. "Not fortune. Magnesium, like in firecrackers and sparklers, eh." He pointed to the throttle. "Shut down boat. We make sure." He waited until the boat was silent, floating. He got matches from the galley, cupped a hand, and struck one of them. He held the strip over the side and lit it. It burst into white-hot fire, violent, throwing off sparks like a fuse. He dropped the burning metal into the lagoon. It turned in circles, sputtered, then sank toward the bottom, still burning.

"It burns underwater?" Maruul said.

"Magnesium is crazy metal," Wally said. "Still not treasure."

They hung over the railing until the burning strip disappeared. PC brushed his shock of hair from his eyes, slid behind the wheel, and opened the throttle wide. The propellers shrieked, rushed the boat forward.

Maruul still thought of the riddle. "What does the last line of the riddle mean—*Dawn the beast will slay*?" she asked.

Wally Wallygong threw open his arms again, this time to a squawking brown gull. "Who knows?" he shouted. "But I bet we find out, eh!"

That night PC checked out the storage drawers and bins on the mooring platform. He found a couple of dive watches with timer buttons. He took one, put it on his wrist. There were several belt knives and an industrial camcorder. A Nikonos-V camera lay inside an underwater shoot bag. He opened the Ziploc, lifted the camera out to check the speed of the lens. He thought of Ratboy and went to get it from the cabana.

The laptop fit easily into the empty transparent shoot bag. He slipped his hands into the pair of gloves molded into the sides of the bag, opened the computer, and turned it on. It worked. Ratboy was going diving.

PC stayed up long after Wally and Maruul had crashed in the skiff bunks. He'd found a box of adapters, and he ran the platform generator to recharge a double set of Ratboy's batteries. He pulled up a program with a list of Australian expressions: "billy tea," tea boiled over an open fire; "bonnet," hood of a car; "dunny," slang for toilet, but really an outhouse; "esky," Styrofoam cooler; "knickers," underwear . . .

The list on Ratboy's screen was long. PC's eyes began to tire. He turned the laptop off. For a while his mind drifted in the shadows of the cabana. He thought about Cliff and Arnhem. The horror of being devoured alive.

And something else. Himself. There were changes going on inside him. Somehow he felt different from when he'd gotten on the plane in

San Francisco. Each sense was alert, processing data in a new way. Images. Waves moving across the reef to slap the pontoons beneath the platform. Fish jumping. He heard a cat's-paw of wind creeping through the sheets of white canvas. Smells. Damp rope. Stinging salt lifting high into his nostrils.

And he found himself thinking of Maruul.

Her hair. The beauty of her face. Her voice. He fell asleep.

It was early in the morning when PC heard the racket. He thought he was seeing things: an old man with dreadlocks shouting and banging a pair of frying pans together.

"I see them! I see them!" Wally cried out.

PC stumbled out of the cabana. Maruul mustered on the skiff. Wally dropped the frying pans, returned to peering through a telescope. "They're at the *Anemone*," he said.

PC rubbed at his eyes. "Who?"

"The Coast Guard! We hurry, eh. Snoop. Nephew and I dive all the time at chalk cliff when Coast Guard visit freighter. Giant clams. Hammerheads. Freighter never make sounds then. Just worry about great white sharks.

Hurry. We kill two birds with one stone and spy on freighter."

PC looked to Maruul. She was excited. He knew the treasure hunt was on.

SIX

INTO THE ABYSS

PC ran the skiff south to the chalk wall, beyond the ledge where they'd lost Cliff, and dropped anchor. The *Anemone* was three hundred yards off in open water. Up close, it looked shabbier, diminished by complete neglect. The antiseptic white Coast Guard craft was moored at the freighter's boarding platform.

Wally Wallygong was the first into his wet suit.

"You're diving?" PC asked. "You think it's okay?"

"I have lungs like crocodile," Wally said. "Kick like boxing kangaroo, eh."

PC searched for bang sticks. There were none. Not even a speargun. Maruul tested her gear. She noticed the laptop in the shoot bag strapped to PC's tank.

"Ratboy's coming with us?"

"Yes."

Maruul checked the water for movement and lurking dark shadows as she climbed onto the stern platform. She dropped into the water, bobbed to the top, and peered out from her mask. Wally and PC regulated their breathers. They spit in their masks to minimize fogging, then plunged in.

The trio stayed close to the chalk wall. Deep. Deeper. Blood-red fans and white brain coral protruded from patch rock. The silver band of magnesium snaked down through the whiteness—down as far as they could see.

Down.

At the bottom, they reached the edge of a dead volcanic mound. Wally led them across the strange seascape where tiny orange and red polyps had begun to thrive, extending the base of the reef. Black-and-yellow-spotted fish peered out from a jungle of undulating seaweed.

Wally slowed his kicking and began turning in small circles. He paused at every shrimp, cuttlefish, and sea cucumber. PC took Maruul's arm, brought his face smack up to hers. "What's he doing?" he said without removing his mouthpiece. She was able to hear and understood his garbled sounds. She stayed close to his ear so he could hear her respond. "Apologizing to the fish for us being here," she said. "Old Aboriginal men—fishermen and hunters—do that."

She watched his face behind his mask. He smiled and waved that he understood.

Wally motioned them to stay clear of a cluster of large speckled eels. "Electric eel fish. Give good shock," Wally said in PC's ear. PC looked closer at their markings. He'd seen electric eels only off Venezuela, but he realized volcanic vents had probably spawned their own.

"Shock in tails," Wally said. "Nephew touch tail by mistake."

PC motioned Maruul past Wally. He knew they needed to cover ground fast if they were going to check out the freighter. A school of large fish cruised near the surface like ghosts against a burning canopy. Maruul pointed up to them.

"Barracudas," PC mouthed.

Maruul understood and shuddered. PC swam on. The freighter's hull was hidden by a curtain of gases rising from volcanic vents. Towering chimneys spewed out plumes of dark minerals and swirling, hot water. Maruul slowed. Wally swam past her. He caught up with PC and showed him something in his hand.

"Clam," Wally said. He took the knife from

PC's belt and began to pry the shellfish open. "Delicious, eh. We eat."

Maruul watched from a distance, annoyed Wally and PC were wasting time trying to eat a clam underwater. She settled down to rest on a rock. A piece of exotic seaweed floated up between her legs and crept around her thigh. She tried to brush it away, but another coarser piece curled around her left calf. She slapped at the weeds, but they didn't budge.

A pillow.

She reached down, felt a puffy, amorphous swelling. She listed slowly to the right and saw that the salt-and-pepper camouflage beneath her was a blob with white, angry eyes. Maruul knew the ugly, living sack wasn't large enough to kill her, but its mouth was nibbling at her diving suit. Its tentacles clung to her legs like giant leeches. She kicked, then swam with the hump of hungry gook clinging to her.

"PC!" she shouted in a burst of bubbles.

Her vision blurred. The vision of Wally and PC was spotty, moving in and out of focus. Her hands struck out to cup the water, to draw her body ahead. Instead, her fingers felt more slime.

Spooky slime.

Jelly.

Shimmering disks the size of dinner plates flowed past her as if she were passing through an aquatic asteroid field. Jellyfish. Her nails ripped into them as they slid across her face. She gasped, managed to scream again—a muted, frustrated sound and blast of bubbles that almost made her lose her breathing tube.

Wally saw Maruul coming fast at them. He grabbed the octopus and yanked it off her with a single, brisk motion. PC helped swat the globs of jelly from her hair and face. "Sorry," Wally kept saying. "Sorry, jellyfish. Sorry, octopus." The panicked octopus fled into the darkness beneath a ledge.

Wally turned PC's attention back to eating the clam.

LOOK BEHIND YOU, a warning ran through Maruul's mind. She turned as a huge, living slab rose suddenly. It soared, an immense black-and-white form shooting up from a pit.

High.

Higher.

She screamed. PC and Wally looked up from the clam. They saw Maruul framed against a giant manta ray as it chased after a cloud of plankton on the surface.

PC smiled. He knew it wasn't a carnivore. Maruul saw the manta's wide mouth and gill strainers. It took her a moment longer to realize it was harmless. Finally, she laughed with PC and Wally at her fear.

Wally moved them on through a forest of towering seaweed that swayed in the current. PC noticed a sparkle, a small object shining brightly from deep in the weeds. He tapped Maruul's leg to signal her he was taking a detour, then swam on.

The glittery object was ahead, appearing and disappearing with the motion of the seaweed. His hands separated the weeds like a wet, sticky drapery.

An earring.

A silver earring in the shape of a snake. It was suspended from the remains of an ear on a dark, half-eaten human head. Suddenly, the mouth of Arnhem's face opened as though the skull was alive. A fat, green eel rolled out like vomit. PC screamed, bubbles exploding from his mask. He let go of the seaweed, and it closed on the rotting death mask.

PC saw Maruul swimming toward him. "What?" she motioned. PC fought to gain control. His heart was pounding, and he felt sick to his stomach.

He shook his head. "Nothing."

Maruul saw the look in PC's eyes, knew that what he had seen was something she shouldn't know about.

PC signaled Wally and Maruul into a huddle. "We need to get aboard the freighter. We've got to know what they're up to."

"How?" Maruul asked.

The light around them began to pulse. They looked up, saw several sea snakes swimming near the surface. Wally smiled. "Sea snakes are poisonous, but only curious. They like silver trim on dive masks. Follow me."

Wally took off kicking, thrusting upward, with PC and Maruul behind him. They crashed through the blinding curtain of volcanic gases. Wally was the first to reach the surface. The *Anemone*'s boarding platform was less than a hundred feet off. He struck out for it, shouting, "Help! Snakes! Help!" Maruul and PC surfaced and caught on to Wally's idea quickly.

"Snakes! Help!" they all kept screaming,

trying to sound truly frightened, as they swam toward the freighter. Suddenly, there were sharp, startling sounds.

Loud.

Earsplitting.

Gunfire.

Maruul and Wally looked up to the railing of the freighter. Six, seven rifles were being fired, shot after shot, raining lead down into the water behind them.

The last shot had been fired by a tall Caucasian woman. She was barefoot, with a skimpy top and blue, long, slit skirt. PC grabbed the edge of the raft and pulled himself up onto the platform. He slid his tank and mask off and shook the water from his hair.

The woman walked down the freighter's crudely rigged boarding ramp, her arms animated like a praying mantis's. "Hello," she said, slinging her still-smoking rifle over her shoulder. "Is anyone hurt?"

"No," PC said. "Thanks."

"Nasty things, those sea snakes." The woman spoke with a German accent. "I take a swim every morning, and they're always pestering me.

You only have to hit one of them, and the others are content for a while devouring it." She gave a wide smile. "I'm Dr. Ecenbarger."

"These are my friends Maruul and Mr. Wallygong," PC said. "I'm Peter McPhee. Everyone calls me PC."

"Well, hello, PC McPhee." She laughed and shook their hands. "Welcome to the *Anemone*. We were just finishing lunch. Is that your diving skiff anchored near the reef?"

"It's my uncle's."

"Oh, is he still down?"

"No," PC said. "He couldn't make it. He's fixing a kayak at his mooring platform."

Dr. Ecenbarger thought for a moment. "Oh, yes. I've seen a platform north of here."

"Uncle's expecting us to bring him back a reef lobster or bass for lunch."

"I see," she said. "This isn't exactly the safest place to sport dive, is it?" Dr. Ecenbarger laughed again. "You must all be exhausted. Come aboard. Have something to drink and eat with us."

PC looked at Maruul, then Wally. Dr. Ecenbarger watched them as they stripped off their wet suits. PC kept the shoot bag strapped on his back as they followed her up the boarding ramp.

"What are we looking for on this barge?" Maruul whispered.

"I don't know," PC said.

"Something fishy, eh," Wally said, and gave them both a wink.

On deck several servants surrounded them. They took the doctor's rifle, then moved like curious, efficient phantoms to dry the visitors with towels. They gave Maruul a robe and offered sandals.

"We're lucky to meet so many new friends today," Dr. Ecenbarger said. Two men in Coast Guard whites relaxed their rifles. A third, an officer, put his pistol away and approached Maruul. "I'm Lt. Roessler. You're the young lady who lost her brother out here last week, aren't you?"

PC stepped between Lt. Roessler and Maruul to field his questions. "That's right, she is," PC said.

The officer turned his gaze onto him. "Terrible accident. Our boat was the one that found her in the kayak. We took her to the mainland. I'm sorry we never found the boy."

Maruul's eyes started to fill with tears, but she got control of herself. She carefully began to examine each face aboard the freighter. She remembered what Wally had said—that someone from her clan was aboard. Someone who knew her village's secrets.

Dr. Ecenbarger pointed to a buffet of sandwiches, fruit, and drinks. "Please, everyone, help yourselves. You must be starving from the dive."

"We're not hungry," Maruul said.

PC began to check out all the equipment visible on the main deck. "The *Anemone*'s a research ship?" he asked the doctor.

"Yes. A bit of a scientific smorgasbord, I'm happy to say," Dr. Ecenbarger said. "We have a few marine biologists. I'm a geologist, myself."

She tilted her head so each strand of her bobbed hair trickled one by one to the left, reforming perfectly. "The Australian government allows us to take small samples from the vents and look into the biology and chemistry of the mounds. In return, we share our results with their scientists. We've done the same thing in Kalimantan—that's Borneo—and the Malay Archipelago." She spotted the shoot bag on

PC's back. "You dive with a computer?"

"Sometimes. I get bored on a dive waiting for the others to finish," PC said. He flashed her a big grin. "I like playing games."

Dr. Ecenbarger grinned back. "What a coincidence. I love playing games too." She hesitated, as though selecting exactly what game she intended to play at the moment. "And you're very lucky. Lt. Roessler's newly appointed to our local Coast Guard station."

"Transferred from Darwin," Lt. Roessler said. "Perth the year before."

"He's requested a tour of my ship," Dr. Ecenbarger said. "You and your friends must join us. Would you like that?"

"Yeah," PC said. "We'd like that a lot."

Two Asian women appeared from nowhere, flanked the doctor, and helped her slip on a white lab smock and pair of high-heeled shoes. She led the way inside the ship and down a steep metal staircase. Lt. Roessler and his men followed. PC and Maruul joined them as a handful of bare-chested crewmen closed in behind them like well-trained Dobermans. Wally trailed, humming.

"You may have noticed we've got a topmast

on deck to hold some wind instruments, our navigation antennae, and radar," Dr. Ecenbarger said, leading them along a hallway.

"What's the portable crane doing topside?" PC asked.

Dr. Ecenbarger's head swiveled like an alert insect's. She stared at PC as though really seeing him for the first time.

"I didn't notice one," Lt. Roessler said.

"What kind of big sample chunks do you lug up with that?" PC pressed.

Dr. Ecenbarger forced her smile. "We don't use the crane. It was a gift to us in Indonesia. We accepted it because we didn't want to insult the government." She stopped at an open doorway. "This is the staging bay. Our water-sampling system and chromatographic equipment. It's all terribly antiquated, but it's all we can afford just now."

"What are the high-pitched sounds we hear coming from your freighter?" Maruul wanted to know.

"Sounds from the *Anemone*?" Dr. Ecenbarger look surprised.

"Yes," Wally said. He gave Lt. Roessler a playful poke in the ribs to get his attention.

"My nephew and I hear strange sounds many times when we dive near freighter, eh."

Dr. Ecenbarger saw curiosity spark Lt. Roessler's eyes. "It's the small thruster motors on our hull," she explained. "They hold the boat's position in deep water."

"No," PC said, enjoying the doctor's discomfort in front of the Coast Guardsmen. "We heard louder sounds than any thruster motors—shrieking—like an industrial drill."

"In that case I don't know." She shot Lt. Roessler a look of amusement. "Unless, of course, you're hearing a siren, the kind the ancient Greeks believed in—part woman, part bird—whose songs lured sailors to their deaths on the rocks." Lt. Roessler laughed with her as she led everyone into a cavernous room at the center of the ship.

A dozen technicians were working with crude microscopes, outdated balances, and setups of titration tubes and retorts. "This is our main lab and specimen room," Dr. Ecenbarger said. There were shelves of yellowing dead snakes, fish, and lizards crammed into gallon jars of formaldehyde.

Maruul noticed a wall of curtains behind her.

She tried to signal Wally to drop back and explore the area with her, but he was busy snooping through one lab cabinet after the next.

The doctor pressed a button, and a computerized sketch of the *Anemone* appeared on several screens throughout the room. The drawing became crudely animated, with red pointers and flashing labels—indicating the crew's quarters, galleys, staterooms, and storerooms.

"As you can see," Dr. Ecenbarger said, "my vessel is an open CD."

Maruul slowly opened the first set of curtains behind her. She saw a mass of bug legs and waving antennae protruding from a screened cage. The screen held back hundreds and hundreds of giant winged cockroaches, their six-inch backs glistening. A creamy fluid oozed from their abdomens. She screamed and yanked her hands back.

Everyone turned to look at her.

"Sorry," she said.

"African cockroaches," Dr. Ecenbarger explained. "Some of our specimens are alive. We use them for tests with the microbes we're finding in the sea vents."

During the commotion, PC moved stealthily

to a computer in a rear corner. He slid Ratboy out of its shoot bag, turned it on, and connected its RF cable to a free port on the ship's computer.

Dr. Ecenbarger's attention was on Lt. Roessler. "Imagine. Life existing at six hundred and eighty-five degrees Fahrenheit! Isn't that exciting?"

"There's gold in the vents, too, isn't there?" Lt. Roessler asked.

"Only traces of precious metals," Dr. Ecenbarger said.

"Ha!" Wally blurted out, like a rude child. The Coast Guardsmen turned to Wally for an explanation. He pretended he only had to sneeze.

HA-CHOO!

"One of the undersea towers is huge." The doctor moved on quickly. "Our divers have nicknamed it 'Gargantua.' We've done analyses on the minuscule samples of rock the government allows us to take. There are richer quantities of copper and zinc, but the ability to commercially mine any minerals is twenty years away."

Wally saw what PC was up to and moved to the other side of the room. "Doctor! Doctor!" he called out. "Do you have lizards? I smell big lizards, eh, eh. I get dizzy. And a rash! I'm getting a rash now, eh! Where are the lizards?" His shouting got everyone's attention, as PC's fingers quickly punched the keyboard and began downloading the *Anemone*'s files. Dr. Ecenbarger rushed over to Wally and spoke to him like he was deaf. "Mr. Wallygong, we have no live lizards. No lizards aboard whatsoever. . . ."

Maruul moved farther along the wall. She flung open another curtain.

At first the cage looked empty, so she stepped closer. Slowly, she became aware of a chattering sound and a fluttering of wings. Maruul glanced down. A mob of hungry black bats was pressed against the bottom of the cage trying to bite her feet.

Dr. Ecenbarger continued to speak over Maruul's latest shrieks. She signaled a heavily muscled guard toward Maruul. "We were given the bats in Bombay. We take pride in keeping our specimens alive as long as possible. Gibraltar presented us with extraordinary primates. They were more difficult to sustain."

"Do you ever cut up monkeys?" Wally asked innocently.

"Why do you ask a question like that?" Lt. Roessler wanted to know.

The doctor's thin red lips twitched, then fixed themselves into a grin as she stared at Wally. "No, we don't cut up monkeys," she said, "Unless it's an autopsy and we need to know why they've died."

PC unhooked Ratboy and turned his attention to what the technicians were doing. They might be using a lot of authentic laboratory equipment—Erlenmeyer flasks, centrifuges, metric weights, lots of gizmos—but something was wrong. They all looked like they were faking experiments. It was as if they were putting on some sort of a *show*.

What PC decided *was* real was the shrewdness in Dr. Ecenbarger's eyes. PC looked at Maruul. We're running out of time, he thought.

PC went to Maruul's side and guided her back along the curtains and away from the muscled guard. They both looked over to where they'd last seen Wally.

"Where is he?" Maruul whispered.

"He's gone," PC said, puzzled.

They noticed Dr. Ecenbarger's eyes shooting about and knew she too was concerned with what had happened to Wally Wallygong. She started winding up for the Coast Guardsmen. "Volcanic vents like the ones here at the Great Barrier Reef were long considered geological and biological wastelands. Instead, we are finding they will one day be of enormous value."

She took Lt. Roessler's arm. As she started to lead everyone out, PC noticed a curtain moving. A breeze had come from somewhere. Another door or a porthole had been opened. He slid the curtains aside, expecting to catch sight of Wally.

Maruul shuddered. PC slipped his hand over her mouth to stifle her scream. The bodies of several large baboons, their mouths snarling in rage at their death, hovered over them like monstrous angels. They floated in yellow fluid inside a glass cylinder.

But Maruul had seen something else, too. A figure—not Wally—dressed in animal skins and wearing a necklace of crocodile teeth. The dark man looked familiar to Maruul as he ran away down a hallway and disappeared.

"Keep moving. You follow doctor's tour." The muscle-bound guard prodded them and pulled the curtains shut again.

"Sure," PC said. It was his turn to fake a smile. He glanced back at the cage of bats. Suddenly, he let his foot fly out and kicked open the latch. The front of the cage sprang down. Hundreds upon hundreds of shrieking, furious bats flew out.

The guard shouted and grabbed at the air. There was the sound of breaking wings.

Dr. Ecenbarger heard the shouting, left her Coast Guard guests, and hurried back into the lab. She saw the cloud of raging, maddened bats attacking her flailing guard. For a moment she was confused. Then she realized that PC and Maruul were gone. Her face contorted with rage. She closed the door and began screaming at the guard.

"You idiot! You stupid idiot!"

SEVEN

SHAMAN

"That was my village's holy man!" Maruul said, running with PC down the hallway where the man with the crocodile necklace had disappeared. "What you might call a medicine man or a shaman."

"I thought some corporation henchmen cut his heart out?"

"They cut out *somebody*'s heart."

PC dragged Maruul through a doorway following the sound of the fleeing footsteps. "He knew about the map?"

"Yes."

They could hear men running behind them, searching for them. The passageway came to an end. There were two doors. PC flipped open Ratboy, brought up the layout of the *Anemone*, and pointed to the screen. "I think we're here." The door on the right was locked. The left one pushed open easily. PC hesitated.

"What's the matter?" Maruul said.

"According to this blueprint, there isn't supposed to be a left door."

"So?"

"It means there's a lot more on this tub of tin than meets the eye."

They went through the left door and ran down a flight of stairs. There was another passageway. Steel sheeting, cables, and spikes were strewn about the length of the hallway. Suddenly, the lights went out.

"I can't see," Maruul yelled. PC turned up the intensity on Ratboy's screen. He checked the deck plans. "This is a place that's not supposed to exist."

Click. Click.

"What's that sound?" PC asked.

"What sound?"

It took PC a moment to figure out what it was.

"Could you keep your hair quiet?" he told Maruul.

"Sorry." She held her beaded braids so they wouldn't knock against each other.

PC tripped, knocking over a pile of long, thin metal pipes. They crashed to the floor. "And you're worried about my hair?" Maruul whispered in his ear.

After the last pipe stopped rolling, they continued forward.

"I'm getting a chill," Maruul said, pulling her robe tighter around herself.

"I've got goose bumps too," PC said.

There was an unidentifiable crackling and sounds of scurrying.

PC tilted Ratboy's screen so it lighted their feet. They were standing on a moving, living rug of twitching little claws. PC and Maruul screamed, jumped up and down, and lost their balance. They reached out to the walls, but their hands sank into more of the moving, brittle shag.

Maruul shuddered. "What are they?"

"Some kind of hairy land crabs," PC said. "Dr. Ecenbarger's a pretty lousy housekeeper."

The crabs pinched their fingers and began to leap onto their bare legs. Now, suddenly, a door opened at the end of the passageway. Silhouetted in the doorway was the figure of the shaman, towering in a horned headdress. Maruul shouted at him in her native language. *"Why have you turned against your village? You're killing our tribe. Killing it!"*

The shaman stayed silent and motionless,

as though daring them to approach him. PC yanked Maruul behind him and ran through the gauntlet of crabs.

They had almost reached the shaman when he turned and ran into another room. PC and Maruul followed him inside and were nearly blinded by floodlights that hung from the ceiling. It was another laboratory—a secret one, not on the ship's blueprints. The shaman retreated to a doorway on the opposite side. When PC and Maruul were in the middle of the room, he stepped through the doorway and slammed the steel-and-glass door closed behind him. PC ran to the door and yanked on its handle. He tried to force it open, but it was sealed shut. Suddenly, across the room, the door they had entered from swung closed, too.

PC turned to Maruul. "This is a trap!" he yelled.

They raced from one door to the other, hitting and kicking at the latches, the glass. The doors didn't budge; the glass was several inches thick. Finally, they stopped pounding and held their hands up to shield their eyes from the floodlights. A computer console was welded to the right wall. Chrome benches and a stainless-steel table were riveted to the floor.

"What is this?" Maruul asked.

"A decompression chamber," PC said. "If a diver comes up too fast from a dive, the nitrogen starts to boil out of his blood. They call it the bends. It's terribly painful, and it can kill you. This chamber builds up pressure to push the gas back into the blood. Then they lower the pressure slowly so the gases in the diver's blood don't come out too fast."

A stench floated toward them, making them choke. Slowly, they became aware of a strange sloshing sound coming from behind the steel table. Closer, the terrible odor became overwhelming. Maruul buried her nose and mouth in the skin of her arm. In front of them, shimmering under the stark whiteness of the lights, was a mass of maggots covering the form of a rotting animal.

"What was it?" PC asked.

"Some kind of a dog," Maruul said. "The shaman's old let's-bite-a-dead-dog trick obviously works around here too!" The thousands of tiny white worms covered the carcass so thickly, it was a rippling, living mass.

Suddenly, there was a hissing sound, like gas

escaping. They looked up to a row of metal ducts on the ceiling. "What's happening?" Maruul asked.

"They're sucking the air out of the chamber."

PC set Ratboy down and charged one of the doors, throwing all his weight behind a solid karate kick. His foot connected, but the glass held strong. He kicked again.

And again.

"I'm getting pains in my chest. I can't swallow," Maruul said.

"We've got to do something fast, or the pressure's going to drop so low that we'll both *explode*," PC yelled. He turned to the computer welded to the wall and typed in a STOP/CANCEL command on the keyboard. A message flashed on the screen: AUXILIARY IN USE. CANNOT OVERRIDE.

There was a popping sound. Maruul thought it was her ears.

Another pop.

And another, as though someone was popping corn.

"What's that!" Maruul yelled.

The sounds were coming faster now, especially from behind the steel table where the writhing, oozing carcass lay. In another moment, Maruul answered her own question.

"THE MAGGOTS ARE EXPLODING!"

"Quick, throw your robe over them," PC ordered.

Maruul pulled off her robe and flung it over the bursting carcass.

PC felt drops of blood start falling from his nose. The air pressure was dropping fast. He kicked at the console and pressed his face against the glass window of the door. Another face—dark and startling—stared back in at him.

"Wally!" PC cried out.

"Help!" Maruul screamed. "Help us, Wally!"

"There's got to be a set of controls out there, Wally. Find it," PC yelled through the glass. "Hurry!"

"What?" Wally said, unable to hear.

Shouting, PC repeated the command. Wally still couldn't get it. PC grabbed Ratboy, threw open its lid, and typed: FIND THE CONTROLS OUT THERE. THERE HAS TO BE ANOTHER COMPUTER! He held the screen against the window.

The pain in Maruul's head was awful, her

eardrums on the verge of bursting. She staggered to PC's side and began to sink to the floor.

"Wally, we're going to die!" PC screamed. He knew the old man could see them, could see the blood coming from PC's nose. See Maruul losing consciousness. Wally looked torn and helpless. He turned from the window and began to walk away.

"Don't go!" PC cried out.

Wally Wallygong kept moving farther back into the darkness. PC's lungs felt as if they were being ripped up through his throat. Maruul's eyes closed. She laid her head down. PC thought her face would be the last thing he would ever see.

There was one more image.

A figure.

The figure of an old dark man running.

Wally coming back, racing toward the decompression chamber. He looked like a phantom, and when he hit the light spill from the chamber, PC saw the long, thin pipe he held high.

Wally Wallygong came faster.

Faster.

Wally let the strange spear fly with a skill

learned many years before.

There was a tremendous implosion of glass and a rush of air into the chamber, as though a whirlwind had struck.

EIGHT

DEMONS

"Coast Guard gone," Wally Wallygong said. "They ask about you. Doctor tell Lt. Roessler not to worry, eh. She said she'll get you to be with your uncle. She must have seen what happened to Cliff."

"Not if I can help it," PC said, gasping.

PC and Maruul took a series of deep, long breaths. They felt oxygen racing back into their blood and strength returning to their bodies. PC's nose had finally stopped bleeding. There were sounds of guards running toward the shattered chamber. PC opened the ship's program on Ratboy, checked the *Anemone*'s design plan again.

"We've got to move it," PC said. He pulled Maruul to her feet and led her and Wally out through the shattered door of the pressure chamber and down a curving metal stairwell.

Maruul was confused. "Shouldn't we be going up?"

"No."

PC took them deeper inside the ship, far below the waterline. They found a vast lighted room, an area that seemed to be part factory, part smelting plant. There were ingot molds and rinse tanks. Extrusion machines. Furnaces. An alcove of diving equipment. The freighter was turning out to be a Chinese puzzle, PC thought—box within box within box.

Wally went straight to an aisle of open crates brimming with shiny metal. "Magnesium. Doctor mining magnesium. Still, not fortune, eh," he said. Off to the side there was a receiving bin of wet, freshly mined metal spilled out from a sluice.

"Why is Dr. Ecenbarger doing all this? Why would she want to kill us?" Maruul asked.

"Greed," PC said. "She's sick, and can never have enough money or power. There aren't any more countries in the world, you know. There are only corporations with two kinds of people: the ad guys and the Dr. Ecenbargers, the ones who call the shots on the whole scam. They're the mutations—monsters who'd cut our noses off and try to kill us for a buck. There are Ecenbargers all over the place now!"

PC headed for the circular pool beside the

dive equipment. White piping with gauges and valve controls covered a wall. Although he'd seen only pictures of them in articles about high-tech nuclear submarines, he recognized the setup as an ocean interface—a tank that allows divers to launch themselves into the sea from inside a ship.

Maruul turned in a slow circle, taking in the whole of the layout. "What is this place?"

"Whatever it is, it's state-of-the-art. This whole nasty freighter is a front for something else." PC held up one of dozens of slick blue diving vests that had built-in breathing-exhalation bags, soda lime canisters, and nitrox tanks. "Rebreathers. They recycle the air. Divers can stay down for hours."

"My nephew sells rebreathers for plenty of dollars," Wally said. He picked up a face mask with a built-in receiver. "He sells these, too. Now we talk better to each other underwater—like fish. Buddy phones. Got walkie-talkie chip. Five hundred bucks a pop."

Sounds of guards.

Closer.

PC noticed a surveillance camera mounted on the ceiling. It turned like radar. "They know we're here. Suit up," PC said. *"Quick."*

He finished first and made sure Ratboy was dry in the shoot bag. He helped Wally and Maruul buckle the loose ends of their gear. For a moment the three of them looked at each other. Maruul's eyes were wide and alert. Wally set all three of their buddy phones to the same channel. They heard him whisper, "Stone, tree, stars, and human—all are one in our hearts."

We're a team, PC thought, smiling as he launched himself down into blackness.

Maruul and Wally followed. For twenty feet the interface tube remained as dark as a well. Then it became larger, transparent. They could see the hull of the *Anemone* and a blazing aura of sunlight crashing into the water surrounding it. A half dozen other tubes dropped from the freighter like so many glistening filaments dangling from a parasite.

"Ecenbarger's got her freighter rigged like a big leech," PC said into the pencil mike of his buddy phone. "She has it drill and suck up anything she wants."

"Maybe suck up the meat for her cheap sandwiches, too, eh eh," Wally said.

Drills were visible in a few of the tubes:

metal spirals turning slowly and carving into the sparkling magnesium lode beneath the *Anemone*. They saw that the magnesium lode extended along the top of a mound and up high into the chalk wall of the reef.

"These drills aren't making that high-pitched sound we heard," Maruul said.

"Right," PC said. "She's probably got some other kind of gizmo for that."

More than a hundred feet below the surface, the divers surfaced in the exit pool of the interface. PC stood, slid off his mask, and tested the air. "We're in some kind of undersea cave," he said.

Wally and Maruul took off their masks. A moan drifted through the space like breath blown into a giant seashell. Strings of burning naked lightbulbs and pipe-and-board scaffolding covered the pitted rock walls.

"What is this?" Maruul wanted to know.

"It looks like a lava tube," PC said. "There must have been volcanoes on the mainland that erupted a long time ago."

"Yes," Wally said. "Giant fingers of hot lava reached out many years ago under the sea, eh. Have lots of spiders. Some tubes are filled with water. Others have air. Doctor fixed this one up with electric lights."

Maruul peered down the length of the long, strange tunnel. "All Aboriginal people are believed to have once sailed from another land. Maybe our Morga ancestors first landed near here and found the lava tubes. Tubes that stretch out like arms. It could be another reason why they painted little hands and fingers on the piece of bark. I feel spirits. The old Morga clan *was* here."

PC noticed a surveillance camera mounted high on a wall. It oscillated. "Dr. Ecenbarger's got spy cameras all around. She and her goon squad probably saw us come down the interface tube and will be coming after us," PC said. He started to climb the stairs of the scaffolding. The others grabbed their gear and hurried after him. Near the top PC led the way off the clattering boards and onto a crude pathway carved into the rock. They stripped off their wet suits. PC kept Ratboy but stowed the rest of their equipment behind a rock in the dark of a hollow.

There were loud hammering, pounding sounds. Rough voices floated toward them as they turned a corner. The wind became musical, cellolike, as it moved through the passage.

PC led them toward a bright light. He reached the end of the passageway first and hid in shadows near the edge of a precipice. Maruul and Wally caught up, flanked him, and froze, staring out at a startling domain. The ceiling of the underwater cave vaulted high, narrowing like the steeple of a cathedral. Jagged stalactites hung down, appearing to be the pipes of a colossal, ghostly organ. Far below, the main floor of the cavern bubbled out, where strands of once-liquid rock had cooled into buttresses and gnarled shapes from a nightmare. It reminded PC of those hollow sugar Easter eggs, the kind he used to peer into as a child and see miniature castles with tiny people, clouds—birds flying across a painted candy sky.

Floodlights at the top of the cave shone down on several dozen workers hammering away at stone with chisels, pickaxes, even drills.

"Are they Aboriginal men?" PC asked.

"No," Maruul said. "They look like they're from Borneo or one of the other islands near the equator."

"What are those stones?"

"Lava rock," PC said.

Wally scratched his head. "Not worth anything. Why they cut that?"

PC pointed to a huge stitched canvas tarp on the far wall of the chamber. It hung, six or seven stories tall, like a shabby drape. He said, "The main event's behind there. That's your village's fortune. Behind the canvas."

Wally nodded. Maruul stepped closer to the edge to get a better look.

A large glass water tank at the edge of a grotto pool on the right began to glow. Just under the surface was what looked like a black steel chair with thick arm and leg straps. The men laid down their tools and turned toward the tank as though it were a holy altar. They appeared nervous and frightened as eerie, flute-like music began to fill the cavern. A vision of hideous beastly forms began to rise from a ridge beyond the tank.

"Oh, my God," Maruul said. She reached out and took PC's hand as a procession of wild dog heads—dingoes with stiff ears and gaping, toothed mouths—marched toward the glass tank.

"They're men in dog skins. Your shaman's really into dogs," PC said.

Two of the dingo men blew into enormous

flutes made from slender hollowed trees. The last figure in the procession was the shaman, startling in a cape of dog skin, and wearing the largest, most ferocious of the dingo heads. His eyes, visible through holes in the dingo mask, shone like a demon's.

The flutes stopped. Suddenly, a series of screams came from a passageway on the right of the glass tank. Three men dragged out the muscled guard PC and Maruul had last seen swatting at bats in the lab. His arms were tied behind his back. He was prodded by sharp, hooked sticks and driven toward the glowing tank of water.

Quickly, a rebreather was forced into the prisoner's mouth. Then he was lifted into the tank and strapped underwater into the metal chair. He struggled as a long, narrow cage was lowered over his head and belted.

Dr. Ecenbarger, wearing her high spike heels, strode in from a separate dark passageway. She pulled her lab coat tight about her and stared into the tank. At the sight of her, the prisoner stopped his struggle.

"What are they going to do to him?" Maruul whispered.

"I don't know." PC stared down at the doctor, watched her head tilting, calculating. Wally was puzzled, too.

The shaman shouted at the terrified workers. He told them the prisoner had failed the doctor. That because of him, there were enemies loose on the ship. Enemies who could hurt the doctor. Hurt everyone. Because of his bumbling, the prisoner had placed them all in danger, and he would have to be punished.

Dr. Ecenbarger moved closer to the glass. She stared down the long cage that had been strapped to the prisoner's face. The petrified eyes of the muscled guard looked back at her, his garbled pleading nothing more than sense-less, noisy air bubbles. The doctor inspected the cage and made certain it was secure. Satisfied, she stepped up onto a platform, reached into the water, and lifted open a door on the top of the cage. Clutching a fish net, she signaled a guard holding a bucket to approach. With a single motion, she scooped out something large and black and dropped it into the far end of the cage.

Maruul squeezed PC's hand tighter. "It's horrible," she said. "What is it?"

"Another freak from the reef, eh," Wally said.

The prisoner closed his eyes from the sting of salt water. After a moment, a series of tapping sounds made him open them again. He strained to see through the water, but there seemed to be nothing except a dark globe shape that was getting larger. It took him a moment longer to realize it was some sort of spider crab.

Slowly, the crab unfolded its legs. It seemed dazed.

Timid.

It's frightened of me, the guard thought with relief. He watched the crab's antennae swishing through the water. Soon, however, its antennae stopped moving and pointed directly at him. Then, slowly, it crept down the length of the cage, toward the warm flesh of the prisoner's face.

Closer, the guard counted ten legs on the crab, each as thick as a man's arm, with a claw on the end that was the size of a fist. The claws tapped, then grabbed at the metal of the cage, moving the body of the crab closer—closer— until its antennae tickled the prisoner's face.

It's only curious about the breathing mask and the bubbles, the guard wanted to believe.

The crab leaned back on its rear legs, waving

its four front legs. Its claws reached forward and began to move gently through his hair. It crawled closer, its black shining eyes staring straight into his. Under its eyes, a thousand tiny bristles began to circulate water through into its mouth.

The guard's breathing quickened.

A claw reached forward and closed around a small clump of his hair. The prisoner shuddered. The crab pulled the clump out, then sucked it into its mouth.

The guard cried out as another claw opened. It reached around and stroked his ear. This time he tried to jerk away, but his head was locked fast in the cage. He screamed. A billow of air burst from his mouth. The bubbles infuriated the crab. Its eyes narrowed. It moved closer and began shrieking.

The giant crab shot its two front claws forward and grabbed hold of two more clumps of the guard's hair. Pincers slowly closed their pliers' grip around his ears. They yanked and cut until the guard's ears pulled loose. Through the red bubbles of another scream, the guard saw the claws delicately release his flesh into the small, powerful jaws of a hair-rimmed mouth.

The crab turned around and crawled off, tapping its way to the other end of the cage.

It's going to let me live, the guard thought. I'm going to live. It's had enough. The blood in the water clouded his vision. He closed his eyes. He believed Dr. Ecenbarger would call it off. She had just wanted to teach him a lesson. They would take the cage off and unstrap him. They would lift him out.

Suddenly, he felt the rebreather yanked from his face. He opened his eyes. The black, marble eyes of the crab were inches from his own. He felt something tickling his bottom lip. The crab's bristles fluttered faster. The tickling of his lip turned to pain. Barbs on the bristles dug deep into his mouth.

He tried to hold his breath against the pain.

The crab sidestepped, as if it was doing a dance. Then, quickly, it was back in his face again. Two of its side legs swung in a wide arc and closed on the bleeding holes where once there had been ears. Claws dug deeper into the soft flesh, scraping the sides of his head down to the white of the skull. The guard tried to cry out, but his face had no lips. His lungs were empty of air. The final thing he saw before he drowned was the crab's front legs shooting toward his eyes.

The guard was dead only moments before the crab began to feast on his brain.

Dr. Ecenbarger signaled an assistant to spear the crab and lift it out of the water. Others unstrapped the guard and pulled him out for the doctor to see.

"What a talented species of crab we've discovered." She laughed as she shook the crab off the spear and walked over to the control console.

The grotto pool next to the tank lit up. A few small clownfish and eels scattered, attempting to hide among the sparse weeds and slick algae that lined the steep sides. The guards tossed the crab and the mutilated corpse into the grotto pool. They drifted slowly down like refuse toward the deep. The doctor threw a second switch.

EEEEEEEE. EEEEE.

The sound.

Maruul looked up at the familiar sound. She knew from the anguish on PC's and Wally's faces that they had watched everything.

"That's the sound again," Maruul said.

PC stared at the ripples near one end of the pool. "So it's not a drill," he said. "It's one of her experiments. She's figured out how to signal the killer fish that it's feeding time—like one of Pavlov's dogs."

They watched the body of the guard slip farther into the deep of the pool. A huge gray shadow began to separate from the blackness. PC, Wally, and Maruul stared in horror as the monstrosity that had devoured Arnhem and Cliff ascended into the light.

The water boiled as the creature opened its damaged jaws, grabbing, biting—sucking the limbs of the corpse into its mouth.

"The bang stick didn't kill it, eh," Wally said.

In a few moments, all traces of flesh were gone, and the monster disappeared back down through a cloud of blood into the darkness from which it had come.

"How could she train that monster fish to kill people?" Maruul wanted to know.

"Sadistic genius," Wally said.

"Right," PC agreed. "She probably didn't train the fish, because it can't be trained. She's smart. She observes any kind of life when she sees it. It probably didn't take her long to realize the fish gets excited when it hears a certain pitch of motor. She did what people do with orangutans when they put them in shows. They're the one kind of primate nobody can train. All that funny mugging and clowning they do, they do naturally. Anybody who works with orangutans knows you just play around with what they like to do on their own. It makes them *look* like they're trained. Ecenbarger figured out the motor makes the big fish crazy, and want to eat anybody around. That's not exactly rocket science."

Wally rocked back and forth, a chant spilling from his lips. Maruul began to weep. "What are we going to do?" she asked.

PC didn't speak. He watched Dr. Ecenbarger below as she waved to a pair of her men on the scaffolding at the top of the huge canvas. They pulled knives from their belts, sliced at a rope. The canvas fell away. There was an explosion of light and color. Reds, golds, blues, orange. A vast wall of stone that seemed to be burning. Stone aflame. Pulsing. Dazzling. Blinding.

"Sunset," Maruul said, remembering her village's treasure song. *"Sunset hides beneath the sea . . ."*

Wally rubbed at his eyes. "Fire opal. Morga treasure is a wall of opal. One big slab of precious stone, eh. It is Morga fortune."

PC felt adrenaline pumping into his blood. He had seen a small opal in one of his mother's rings. He'd seen others on display in museums, where he'd learned that opals were as valuable as diamonds and usually found only far inland in long-dry ancient seabeds.

Wally whispered, "This very special opal. Sacred slab."

Staring at them were hundreds of figures painted on the towering wall of opal. Paintings of ancient people. Spirits. Kangaroos. Cranes. And everywhere, fish. They all appeared to be alive. Creatures real and imagined. A huge python was painted x-ray style to show its anatomy. A school of barramundi, giant perch, swirled up across the vast middle of the mural. Strange beings and other huge animals glared out of the wall. Images in red and yellow ocher and gold.

"This is *our* dreaming," Wally told Maruul. "Look at the history of your people."

Maruul couldn't speak. For the first time, she truly felt that the religion of her village's elders—the beliefs of Wally—were real. Wally heard cries from the past. The sounds of Marrawuti and of Lightning Man. The Great Serpent. And music. Music that made his heart dance.

"What do the paintings mean?" PC asked.

"They are the wisdom of my people," Maruul said. "They have painted their wisdom to help all who need it." She pointed to the top right side of the wall, a progression of painted images and scenes. "They have drawn the secret lore of hunting and the dangers of badlands."

"They warn of quicksand and show the way to game trails, eh," Wally said.

"And they tell what monsters to avoid," Maruul said, pointing to the lower half of the opal slab, where horrible beasts and sharks rose from the depths of the ocean. What looked like the white spirits of smiling children were painted to look as though they were floating up between the monsters toward the sun.

"Are they supposed to be ghosts?" PC asked.

"I think they're hunters covered with white clay," Maruul said.

"White clay protect Aboriginal people, eh," Wally said. "White clay always part of sacred ceremonies."

At the base of the opal slab, Dr. Ecenbarger spoke to the shaman. He roared her commands out at the workers. "The Coast Guard, and others, will come back. We have little time. You will return to the ship and rest while we bring down the wall. After, you will return, work all night to load. We sail in the morning."

Dr. Ecenbarger exited quickly down the ridge behind the torture tank. The shaman followed her with the guards and dingo-head men.

"They're going to blow up the wall," Maruul said.

Wally watched the workers abandon their tools and move off down the tunnel. He began to weep. "They kill our dreaming. Kill it."

PC stood and looked across to the dazzling wall. For a moment he thought of Cliff, of his mother and father. Grandma Helen. He thought of his life back in San Francisco, and an aching emptiness raced through him. But there was something else. A determination stirred inside him from a hidden corner. He looked at Maruul and Wally and realized he was needed.

He and his new friends would make a plan. They would give back to the Morgas what was theirs.

And they would somehow bring back the Coast Guard to stop Dr. Ecenbarger.

Punish her.

Fix her.

PC signaled Maruul and Wally not to move from the shadows until the last of the workers had disappeared. He turned on Ratboy and searched its encyclopedia for "rocks/minerals." He found what he wanted:

Opal: trigonal/hexagonal. $SiO_2 \cdot nH_2O$. Scatters light. Millions of tiny spheres of noncrystalline quartz. These spheres reflect and scatter light to give opal a play of colors. Precious gemstone.

Maruul's gaze was locked on the huge slab

of opal and its paintings. "A small piece from the opal wall would save my village," she said. "That's what the elders would want me to bring back." She looked to Wally, then to PC.

"Yes. Even little piece worth plenty," Wally said. "Much dollars. Maybe two million, eh."

"We're getting it," PC said.

"What about the doctor?" Maruul asked.

"If she tries to stop us, I kabob her," Wally said.

PC walked farther out onto the high ledge. To the left it dropped in steps like a terrace. Maruul and Wally followed PC down until they reached the tunnel floor. They approached the great slab of opal. Maruul picked up a few shimmering chunks of opal that had broken off from the base of the wall. "These will be enough for my village," Maruul said. "Enough for all of us."

She gave the pieces to PC to put into the bag with Ratboy.

A sound came from behind them. They turned.

Nothing.

"I feel someone watching us, eh," Wally said.

"Only spirits," Maruul said, looking up at the

brilliant paintings. For a few moments the three of them stood amazed at the shining history of a people.

"I don't want to leave this sacred place," Wally said.

"We must go back and get our rebreathers," PC said.

Maruul put her arm around Wally. "He's right," she said.

PC led them down the tunnel toward the interface tank.

More sounds as they neared a bend.

Scuffling.

Grunting.

The noises were coming from the blackness of passageways and alcoves in the tunnel's walls. At first PC thought it almost sounded like wind whirling past the stalactites. Maruul started to run ahead. PC and Wally jogged to keep up with her. PC felt the weight of the opals on his back. They jiggled and bounced against Ratboy in the shoot bag.

Suddenly, a horrendous, hairy face rose up from behind a stone. Maruul screamed. A huge mouth opened, its yellow fangs and saliva bursting from black, stretched lips. The grotesque face and body lunged toward Maruul, his arms swinging and grabbing at the air. A roar erupted from his mouth.

"A baboon!" PC yelled. "This one's alive!"

Maruul froze.

Wally and PC grabbed her, pulled her away from the raging primate. The trio ran still forward. Other screeching baboons vaulted out from other niches and passageways. The maddened, howling animals surrounded them, screaming like inmates in a madhouse.

"What are live baboons doing here?" Maruul asked.

"One of Dr. Ecenbarger's jokes," PC said. "She probably makes pets out of them while she experiments on them. Animals trust her. She knows how to zero in on their instincts and twist them for her amusement. Baboons are easy to train. They don't know she's going to eventually inject them with some kind of new microbe or toxic waste and cut out their brains. She's a real sicko."

A shrill diabolical laugh cut across the din.

Dr. Ecenbarger stepped from an alcove, flanked by the shaman and the dingo-headed guards. "Here, Ko Ko," Dr. Ecenbarger called to the largest baboon. Her pet let out a series of short, joyful shrieks and ran for the doctor. He leaped up into her waiting arms. "Ko Ko is such a good little monkey," the doctor said. She turned to confront PC. "How nice to see you again, PJ."

"*PC*," PC corrected.

Several of her guards wore gas masks. They stepped forward clutching canisters with nozzles. "As I told you on the tour, PC," Dr. Ecenbarger said, petting Ko Ko, "we take pride in keeping our experimental specimens alive as long as possible. As long as possible . . ."

She stepped back as an orange-colored gas burst from the nozzles. It smelled sweet and sickening, like a strong perfume. PC felt it burn his eyes. Wally and Maruul covered their faces. For a few moments, they staggered, and then slowly dropped to the ground. PC thought about resisting—about kicking, punching—but his knees started to buckle, and his mind went blank.

Maruul woke up on chilled, dark metal. Her eyes opened. There were shadows. Terrible smells. She jerked to a sitting position and felt bars of cold steel surrounding her. Hands grabbed at her through the bars. Stroked her. Hairy hands. She was locked in a cage! Other cages holding baboons were stacked beside her on a cart.

"Help! PC! Wally!" she tried to call out, her voice muted by the effects of the gas. Several baboons imitated her panic, screeching, lying on their sides. They made fitful sounds, short comical noises, as they kept reaching into the cage, gently poking at her. One of them, Ko Ko, slid his hand in from behind her. He played with the beads in her hair.

Maruul slapped the baboon's hand. "Stop it." The baboon whimpered, pulled his arm back into his own cage, and stared at her. She grabbed the door of her cage, rattled it as hard as she could. A steel Medeco lock held firm.

BAM BAM BAM

Sounds of a pneumatic drill.

Maruul looked across the cavern to the opal wall. A dozen workmen were crisscrossing scaffolding, drilling, framing the wall with two-inch holes and seeding rods of dynamite into them. She looked for PC and Wally. Where *are* you? What have they done with you?

They weren't in any of the cages, and she couldn't see anyone on the dark, high terraces. The lights of the grotto pool and torture tank were off. *They're going to blow up the wall. They're drilling holes to blow up the wall!*

She tried concentrating on PC. She remembered when she'd first met him that day outside the hospital. This boy could be a friend, she had thought. But now that he was in danger, she realized she wanted him to become more than a friend to her.

She saw a glow start filling the cavern. The lights came up higher, stronger. Soon the tank by the grotto pool was blazing.

A sudden chill grabbed at her throat. Now there were *two* metal chairs in the torture tank.

Maruul threw her weight against the door of the cage. It still wouldn't budge. Ko Ko rattled his cage and tried to pull at the lock. Maruul collapsed, tears streaming from her eyes. The baboon watched Maruul through the bars of his cage. He saw her eyes searching, looking down at all the loose stones.

Stones.

• • •

PC awoke in blackness. His mind struggled against the numbing toxins of the gas. As he fought his way into consciousness, he realized he was bound, gagged, and blindfolded. A damp, putrid smell cut into his nostrils. He heard voices. Men shouting. Words he didn't understand.

The voices were closer now.

Arms lifted him up. He was prodded, pushed to hobble and crawl along on his elbows and knees. The space through which he moved was dark and narrow. He could barely breathe. Soon he was lifted again and thrown onto a platform. He heard the racket of wheels. Felt the vibrations of a cart.

After a while, the uproar and shaking stopped and he was made to stand upright. The tape was ripped from his eyes. The first thing he saw was Wally strapped underwater in one of the torture chairs. Wally sucked in air from a rebreather and stared out at PC.

"Let him go," PC tried to yell through his gag. He struggled to break loose from the guards. The shaman, towering, menacing in his dog-skin cloak, blocked him. He roared PC into silence.

PC strained to look about. He saw men drilling, wiring, high on the opal wall. The lights in the grotto pool. More guards by the tank.

"I didn't kill her, if that's what you're worried about," came Dr. Ecenbarger's voice. The doctor moved into his view, a stethoscope hanging from her neck. "I don't waste anything. The Aboriginal girl is very attractive. I know a number of entrepreneurs who'll pay well for an exotic human toy."

PC tried in vain to remove the tape from his mouth. The guards' viselike grip tightened. Dr. Ecenbarger moved closer and placed the end of the stethoscope against his chest. She listened to his lungs, his breathing. "Good. You're physically quite fit, aren't you?"

Dr. Ecenbarger continued, speaking softly, scientifically, as she examined him. "There are other illnesses that have brought you to us, however. Greed. Pride? Trespassing. I'm sure you're pleased to have disturbed Lt. Roessler. Oh, the Coast Guard left. They pretended to be satisfied. But Lt. Roessler will think about you unruly children. It'll work itself over and over in his brain for a day or two until something will strike him as odd.

"He'll think about my poor, irregular freighter with the strange sounds you brought to his attention. It was a bit of an accident that I stumbled onto the effect a high-pitched frequency has on that large, ugly fish. Yes, something will make Lt. Roessler snoop further. He'll stop by your mooring platform. There will be no one there. He'll come back looking for me and my freighter. This is what officers in the services do. They're trained to inspect. To hover. To lurk about like a pestilence knowing someone, somewhere, is outsmarting them. . . ."

"READY!" a foreman high on the scaffolding called down to the doctor. He held a radiophone to his ear.

The doctor turned from PC and waved up to him. "Tell them on the ship we want an hour and a half," Dr. Ecenbarger said. "Ninety minutes before we blow the wall." She reached her hand to her digital watch and turned to look up at one of the surveillance cameras mounted on a wall. She pressed the timer.

PC tried to work his wrists loose. He managed to cross his right hand over his left wrist. He found the timer button on his dive watch and pressed it.

He struggled to speak.

"What is it?" Dr. Ecenbarger asked. "You wonder what I'm going to do with you? An opal wall with its prehistoric paintings intact *would* have been priceless. Thanks to you, I will have to be satisfied with mere millions upon millions of dollars' worth of smaller clusters. That's all that will be left after the explosion." Suddenly, she slapped him across the face hard—then harder still.

It took her a moment before she could manage her smile again. She moved the cold metal end of the stethoscope back onto his chest.

"You have a fine, strong heart," she said. She signaled the guards. They closed in on him, ripped the tape off his mouth, and forced a tube from a rebreather into his mouth.

"We have time for a couple of final experiments involving the toxicity of mutant sea life on this reef," Dr. Ecenbarger said. "I find it always exciting to discover new poisons. For the old man, I've picked a rather simple creature. Something pedestrian." Dr. Ecenbarger laughed. "For you—well, for you, I've picked the Catch of the Day."

• • •

Maruul watched from her cage across the cavern. She saw the guards lift PC into the tank and strap him underwater in the torture chair next to Wally's chair. She had managed to slide one of her thin shoulders through the bars. She reached down and stretched to touch one of the stones on the floor of the tunnel. She flicked the rock toward her, trying to get a grip on it.

Ko Ko slapped her hand.

"Help me, you monkey," Maruul said, glaring.

The baboon cocked his head.

For a moment, Maruul thought he understood.

Ko Ko reached out, traced his fingers down her arm.

His arm was longer, his hairy strong fingers able to play with the stone. He managed to make it roll farther away.

PC shivered in the cold water. He turned and looked at Wally Wallygong. Wally's eyes were bloodshot. They were saying, "I apologize. Please forgive me. Sorry to you."

CLANK.

The guards strapped a pair of long cages onto

the prisoners' faces. PC stared down the length of his cage. He saw Dr. Ecenbarger and the shaman looking back at him. The doctor's smile had faded. PC tried to talk to her, to make himself understood through the rebreather. She laughed and climbed onto the platform bordering the tank.

An assistant walked up to her with a bucket. The doctor threw open the top of the cage strapped to Wally's face, scooped a fish from the bucket, and dropped it in.

Wally believed it was perhaps one of the most beautiful fish he had ever seen, small and narrow, with photophores on its belly. Its mouth was like a straw, and the sides of its body were covered in bright orange and red stripes. It's lovely like an angel, he thought. The fish paused for a moment, as though shy. Then it saw Wally and swam quickly toward his face.

The fish stopped below his chin and rubbed its long nose on his neck. It felt nice, a little tickly. Wally managed to move his head a little and frightened the fish away. The fish stopped three feet from his face, then turned back to confront him. Wally noticed the fish was breathing much faster now. Suddenly it became huge, puffed like a blowfish, with great needle spikes sticking out from all around its body.

What the devil are you, eh? Wally wondered. A burst of bubbles from his rebreather rose over his face. Suddenly, the fish raced toward him.

Wally thrust his head back, trying to get away, but the fish smacked into him at the base of his neck. Swimming to the surface, it dragged its spikes upward. It was as if a dentist had driven a dozen injections of burning poison up high into the left side of Wally's face. The rebreather stayed strapped tight to his mouth.

Dr. Ecenbarger permitted the fish another moment of violent thrusting before she drove a spear through its body. Then she flipped the fish back into the bucket.

PC fought against his bindings. He shouted and cried out as the fish's venom hit Wally's nervous system.

Wally's body convulsed and strained against the restraints of the chair. As the convulsion passed, he thought only of the opal wall. He remembered the painted barramundi and the python. The ocher beasts and white spirits of smiling children. He had glimpsed his people's

Genesis, and it had been glorious.

Finally, Wally's eyes closed and his body fell limp.

This time Maruul managed to push her shoulder farther through the bars of her cage. She felt her skin tearing, the tendons of her arm stretched painfully. Ko Ko watched her. He grunted, pressed his drooling lips on her shoulder. With one of his long, dangling arms, the baboon easily rolled a stone closer.

Closer.

Dr. Ecenbarger smiled at the look of terror on PC's face. "Don't worry, I'll give the old man a proper burial. In fact, I've already planned his epitaph—'Something fishy.' "

She moved closer to him, staring deep into his eyes. "Your headstone will need quite a different inscription. Perhaps 'He loved to play games.' " She laughed and called for another bucket, and dropped its contents into the cage strapped to PC's face.

The bubbles cleared, and PC saw something move. He looked up to see a large snail about a foot long, with a black-and-white-encrusted shell. It looked like one of those large shells tourists buy in airports, thinking they'll look nice in their bathrooms when they get home.

The snail glided gracefully along the floor of the cage toward PC, leaving a shiny mucus trail behind it. The snail stopped for a moment, as if to take a closer look, before it came forward and climbed slowly up onto his head. PC could feel the muscles of the slimy creature rippling on his skin. It traveled leisurely across his forehead and back down to his neck.

PC tried to shake the snail off, but its grip only got stronger. He watched the head of the snail appear over his chin. He froze. The rest of its fleshy, amorphous body extended far out of its shell and began to slip beneath the rebreather. Soon its slime entered PC's mouth and began to inch down his throat.

PC tried to bite it, but the snail's grip tightened like steel around his chin and jaw. He watched as a long, thin piece of the snail's skin moved out from the shell to reveal a small mouth lined with tiny teeth. The rebreather fell loose from PC's face, and his nose filled with the mucus of the snail. In the short time he could hold his breath, he felt his cheeks bulge as the snail's mouth shot forward inside his own and bit the back of his throat.

The snail hung on ferociously while PC choked uncontrollably as his lungs screamed for oxygen. Then PC felt the first effects of the snail's venom. A dull pain started in his stomach. It crawled upward like a burning acid until he felt a lightness snaking into his brain.

Before he could drown, he experienced a calm. A peace spreading quickly through his body.

His pulse slowed.

A moment later, he felt his heart stop in death.

TEN

THE DARKNESS

Maruul cried as she watched the guards lift PC's body from the torture tank. Dr. Ecenbarger placed her stethoscope against his chest. She smiled at the shaman and her assistants. "What a talented little sea snail," she said. "One bite from it, and he's dead."

The doctor motioned guards to unstrap Wally's body. They lifted it out of the tank and held it for the doctor's examination. She put her stethoscope on his throat and pressed it on an artery.

"This one's still alive," she said disappointedly. She gave a nod toward PC's corpse. "Get rid of them both. Fish food."

The guards tossed the bodies into the grotto pool. Dr. Ecenbarger checked her watch. She gave a signal to the assistant on the control console. He flicked a switch.

EEEEEEE. EEEEE.

Dr. Ecenbarger laughed at the sight of the bodies as they slipped beneath the surface. She turned and, with the shaman and dingo-headed guards, walked down the main passageway. The men from the scaffolds had finished loading their gear onto wheelbarrows and started pushing them back down the tunnel. Other men grabbed the harnesses of the cartful of monkey cages.

The baboons shrieked. Ko Ko watched Maruul making a last reach for a stone. Finally, as if he knew he'd teased her long enough, he rolled a stone into her hands.

Maruul grabbed the stone and began smashing the lock on her cage.

Hard.

Harder.

The wailing animals and the racket of the wheelbarrows and carts masked the sound of her blows. On the third smash, the lock sprang open. Maruul leaped off the moving cart and ran into the deep shadows along the wall. She raced back to the grotto pool. She saw the two bodies slowly drifting downward toward the darkness at the bottom of the pool. Grabbing PC's abandoned rebreather, she dove into the pool. The salt burned her eyes.

EEEEEEEE.

Maruul sucked air from the mouthpiece.

EEEEE. EEEE.

Down.

Down until she reached PC. His face was frozen, his eyes open and startled in death. She trembled as she took the air tube from her mouth and brought the stream of bubbles to his lips. *Your heart didn't stop. Please! Wake up. Wake up.*

PC didn't take any air. She yanked the tube back to her own mouth, took a deep breath, and slid her hand under PC's chin. She kicked, thrust upward as hard as she could. It was not enough. They still fell toward the darkness below.

Wally's body had drifted to the side of the grotto pool. A ribbon of plants and rocks slowed its descent. Pulling PC along with her, Maruul swam toward Wally. She got a footing on a ridge. She tried again to make PC breathe some air.

What would you do, PC? she wondered. You'd probably turn on your computer, Ratboy, to find something for a heart that had stopped.

Something.

She put the air tube back into her mouth and

beat at his chest. The water weakened her blows.

Seaweed undulated beneath her feet. Clownfish stared. Amazed. Disturbed. Near them, Maruul saw a cluster of speckled eels.

Electric eels.

Maruul pushed PC's body toward the rock wall. His skin bruised and tore against a strip of coral. The eels turned in warning. Maruul pushed PC closer until his body touched them.

A tremendous flash was discharged from the tail of one of the eels, a sparking shaft of light passing from the fish into PC's body. Maruul tried to pull her hand away, but the charge radiated through PC's body. She felt the jolt thrusting her backward. She recovered quickly and pulled PC toward her. Her eyes searched his face. A small bubble formed at his lips. A single bubble.

Then others.

Suddenly, PC's body shuddered.

A burst of air shot from his mouth; then he began to choke. She jammed the air tube into his mouth. His chest heaved, his eyes opened. She saw life rushing back into his body, watched consciousness crawl into his eyes.

He came back from death and saw her.

The tube.

He understood.

PC began to kick.

Then he looked around and saw Wally, slowly sliding deeper.

EEEEEEE. EEEEEEEE.

PC heard the sound. He saw something huge rising from the blackness beneath them. He pushed the air tube toward Maruul's mouth and pointed up. She understood. She took a deep breath, gave him back the rebreather, then kicked for all she was worth toward the surface.

PC stuck the rebreather tube in his mouth and swam for Wally. He slid his hands down Wally's limp, unconscious body, found a firm grip, and started to swim with him up toward the light.

The monstrous fish was rising fast into the light. For a moment, it seemed confused by all the kicking and splashing in the pool. By the time it had locked onto its prey, PC had hit the surface. Maruul was waiting, her hand outstretched. She pulled PC out of the water onto the ledge, then together they lifted Wally out of the pool. The fish swam in circles for a moment, churning the water violently, then dove back to the cover of the deep.

"Wally!" Maruul cried. "Wally!"

PC rolled him onto his back and pressed hard on his lower chest. Water and spittle poured out of Wally's mouth. PC held Wally's nose, put his mouth over the old man's mouth, and breathed air into his lungs.

Again.

And again.

Wally began to cough.

"The poison's wearing off," PC said. "It's wearing off."

Wally opened his eyes. He looked at PC and then at Maruul. Slowly, a smile crept onto his face. "Lungs like a crocodile, I told you," he said hoarsely. "Lungs like a crocodile . . . eh."

For a while, the three of them just sat gasping and holding on to each other. They looked at the slab of fire opal that towered above them. A mass of crimson and gold creatures and spirits. The painted wisdom of a people's dreams. PC thought of Cliff and Arnhem and wished they could have seen it.

The high-pitched sound had stopped. The

clamor of animals and men brought them to their feet.

Maruul saw a shining crumple of plastic. The guards had left the shoot bag! She ran to it. Ratboy and the clusters of opals were still inside. She brought the bag to PC and helped him strap it on his back.

"What are we going to do?" Maruul asked.

PC checked his dive watch. "They're blowing the wall in forty minutes. We've got to get out of here."

Wally was still shaky on his feet. He turned slowly to take a last look at the blazing sacred wall. PC led the way into a narrow tunnel. Ahead they saw the gang of workmen unloading their gear and carts. Others had already suited up and plunged into the interface pool to return to the ship. The baboons still howled and shrieked in their cages.

PC signaled Maruul and Wally to stay in the shadows against the wall of the tunnel. "There's got to be more than one way out of here," PC said. "A VIP way Dr. Ecenbarger and her head honchos use. Did you see her heels?"

Somehow, Ko Ko spotted Maruul and began to whimper and bang on the door of his cage. Wally sniffed at the air and put his hand up to feel which way the wind was blowing. "Baboons must know a way out of here. They cannot come by the water tube. This lava tunnel has wind. It is open to air somewhere on an island, eh."

"Set them loose," Maruul said. "If we don't let them out, they'll end up in one of the doctor's pickle jars. Besides, maybe they'll help us."

"Baboons are crazy. Very strong and very nuts," Wally said. "I have one rule—never depend on a monkey, eh."

PC spied the iron head of a pickax. He picked it up and crept alongside the baboon cart, keeping out of sight of the workers. He broke the lock on a chain that had been threaded through the cage doors. Maruul and Wally pulled the chain free and threw open the cages. Ko Ko leaped onto the floor of the tunnel. The rest of the baboons followed.

Workmen tried to stop the escaping baboons, but the baboons were faster. They screamed, bared their teeth, and climbed up the scaffolding. Soon heavy boards and pipes rained down on the men's heads.

PC ran ahead, leading Maruul and Wally past the chaos.

"Look! There's something down here!" Maruul and Wally caught up to PC. He stood in front of a transparent plastic wall.

Below them, a small portable crane lifted a heavy steel cylinder ten feet into the air, then dropped it like the weight on a pile driver.

"What is it?" Maruul asked.

PC said, "The machine crushes the big chunks of magnesium, then conveys the magnesium shards up into the ship." The steel cylinder was lifted again, dropped, and hammered another load of the silvery metal. A blizzard of shredded, pulverized magnesium whirled, filled the transparent enclosure, then was drawn up toward the belly of the freighter.

"Like a big blender, eh," Wally said.

Suddenly, there was a swirl of black dingo skin rushing out from the shadows of the tunnel. Maruul screamed. PC and Wally spun around. The eyes of the laughing shaman blazed down from his canine shroud. He was flanked by two of his dog-headed henchmen.

The shaman knocked Maruul aside and charged PC. PC aimed a kick at the shaman's stomach, but he swatted PC's leg away as if it was a stick. Maruul and Wally crashed into the dingo guards and broke past them out into the main tunnel.

A foot taller and twice PC's weight, the shaman roared, grabbed PC, and tried to bend him over backward. Pain stabbed PC's spine as he punched at the dog-faced maniac. He thrust his head into the shaman's head. The shaman cried out, grabbed PC by his shoulders, and hurled him against the railing of the crusher.

One of the dingo guards took out after Maruul. She dodged around stalagmites and drill equipment. He caught her, yanked her around, and backhanded her across her face.

Maruul cried out in pain. She turned to run again, then spotted a shovel leaning against the wall. She grabbed it and swung it with all her strength into the guard's groin. The guard staggered backward. She brought the shovel back up and cracked him on his head. He dropped in his tracks.

Maruul heard Wally shouting. She ran back to the recess and saw a dingo head pinning him to the ground, clutching the old man's throat.

"No!" Maruul shouted as she ran, swinging

the shovel upward. While the guard was looking up at Maruul, Wally's hands shot above his head and grabbed a stone. He smashed it into his attacker's head.

Again.

And again.

PC rolled on the ground, trying to get away from the crusher. But the shaman caught him by the arm and threw him against the safety railing, shattering it. Pieces of the wooden railing slid down to mix with the chunks of magnesium. The huge steel cylinder lifted, sucked the wood and metal into the crushing chamber, and dropped.

BAM.

The pieces of wood and magnesium were a solution of shreds sucked up out of sight.

The shaman grabbed PC by his feet, thrust him over backward, and began shoving him head-first toward the gaping mouth of the crusher. PC felt a vacuum as the cylinder lifted. He fought against being pulled into the machine. The shaman smiled as he lifted PC's legs, pinning his shoulders down. He began to slide PC in.

BAM.

The cylinder socked down just beyond PC's head. He felt shards of magnesium cutting into his back, and a rush of air as the piston lifted again.

"Let go of him! Let go of him!" He heard Maruul and Wally yelling, trying to pull the shaman off. Suddenly, PC kicked his legs free and wrapped them around the neck of the shaman. The shaman stopped laughing as PC yanked him over, headfirst, toward the crusher. The shaman felt a flutter in his dog-skin cape as the cylinder rose. He tried to pull away from the vacuum, but the cape was sucked in and he along with it.

PC sprang to his feet in time to hear the shaman screaming out from behind the transparent wall. Maruul covered her eyes.

BAM.

One moment, there were shreds of flesh and bone crushed into the bed of magnesium. The next, all was red and silvery—death being sucked up into the *Anemone*.

PC pointed in the direction from which the shaman and the dingo-headed guards had appeared. "That must be another way out of here." He began to run, with Maruul and Wally fast behind him. The tunnel dead-ended at another grotto pool. Diving gear and several battered but streamlined submersibles lay ready at the pool's edge.

"The Executive Lounge," PC said. He ran to one of the submersibles. "This is how Doctor Ecenbarger and her top dingo boys travel back and forth to the freighter. VASH subs with closed cockpits."

"What's VASH?" Maruul asked, checking out the diving equipment.

"Stands for *v*ariable *a*ltitude *s*ubmersible *h*ydrofoil," PC said. "They can travel on top of and under the ocean." He checked out the diving gear, grabbed three rebreathers, and tossed them onto the floor of the sub.

There were sounds of guards heading down the tunnel toward them as the trio fastened their gear. PC slid in behind the controls of the sub, found the magneto switch, and started the engine. Maruul squeezed in behind him.

"Hurry, Wally," PC shouted.

"Sardines in can," Wally said, squeezing in after Maruul.

PC cruised the submersible around the edge of the pool. A dozen guards and dingo men ran toward them with guns drawn. They started to fire.

"Duck," PC yelled.

Bullets ricocheted off the grotto walls. PC held one hand on the steering wheel of the sub; the other grabbed for the dive-flap control. He opened the throttle wide, slid the canopy into place, and dropped the flaps. The VASH sub dove below the surface. The single nose head-light gave off a shaft of laser-bright light that burned through the darkness of a tunnel.

"Too fast," Maruul yelled.

"That's all these babies do," PC said. "Fast."

He brought the throttle back, but the craft began to shoot upward, slicing off several of the hanging tips of stalactites.

"Find bigger flooded lava tube, eh," Wally shouted.

"I'm trying," PC called out.

The sub shot through the flooded tunnel, racing around one curve and then another. The walls started to narrow. PC tried to hold the speeding sub to the center, but it began to scrape and bounce off the walls. Suddenly, the narrow tunnel gave way and they shot out into a wider section of the underwater labyrinth.

"Oh, no," Maruul said, seeing a half dozen lights in the passageway they had just come from. "They're after us."

Wally turned in his seat. "Dingo heads."

A long, thin object headed for them.

Whooooosh.

It flew by.

"Dingo heads with spearguns," Maruul added.

Wally saw shining cylinders rotating on the sides of their attackers' subs. "Spear *machine* guns," he said.

"I had to pick a sub without any!" PC said. He looked at a radar screen on the control board. He saw the trail of spears closing fast.

Whoooooosh. Whooosh.

He turned the sub sharply into another tunnel, and the spears missed. But the *lights* followed. The attackers were only two to a sub. Faster.

Much faster.

The tunnel began to narrow again. PC slalomed between a row of pinnacles and rocks. Ahead he saw the roof of the tunnel appear to break away. He slapped the front flaps up.

"What are you doing?" Maruul screamed.

The sub angled upward. Higher. Higher.

Suddenly, it shot ten, fifteen feet into the air, then fell back down into the water. Maruul screamed. Wally saw a shower of aluminum spears break the surface and fall wide of their mark.

Wally laughed. "We not easy target, eh."

One of the attackers' subs surfaced and went airborne into a rock. The craft exploded like a bomb, sending the flaming torsos of its driver and gunner flying through the air.

"Oh, God," Maruul said. Then another sub shot up and landed close to them.

PC got the hang of diving and jumping. He gave the VASH sub another leap. And another. For a moment he believed he could outmaneuver the dingo heads.

"Dead end!" Maruul cried out.

PC yelled too when he saw the tunnel wall. He yanked at the steering wheel as he sent the submersible upward. It shot out of the water, twisting, turning a hundred eighty degrees. The engines screamed in air. The sub slowed, hovered, then dropped headfirst like a fish. One of the attackers' subs flew over PC's, hit the dead-end wall, and burst into a fireball. PC opened the throttle again. The sub leaped forward as the other subs raced at him on a collision course. PC dodged them. Spears ricocheted off the sides of the sub.

"I WANT THEM KILLED!" Dr. Ecenbarger shouted in the control room of the *Anemone*. She threw a switch. A sound machine—identical to the one at the grotto pool—was mounted below the waterline of the freighter. It began its high-pitched shrieking. She had watched the images of the three intruders on the monitors. She saw them climb into a VASH sub and disappear into the flooded maze of the lava tubes.

She knocked one of her lab assistants out of the way and looked up to a digital readout on the electronic detonator that would set off the dynamite in the opal wall.

Eighteen minutes, twenty seconds . . . Eighteen minutes, nineteen seconds . . .

EEEEE. EEEEEEEE.

Her eyes welcomed the dark shadow moving across the screen of one of the monitors. She bit gently on her lower lip and smiled.

ELEVEN

FINAL BLOOD

"They're gone," Maruul said. "No dingo heads."

PC checked the rearview mirrors on the craft and saw nothing. He eased back on the throttle. But a new blip appeared on the control panel's sonar screen. "The sonar says there's something behind us," he said. "Something coming fast."

"Does our sub have rear spotlight, eh?" Wally asked.

PC looked at a cluster of levers next to the headlight switch. He flicked each of them on and off until he hit one that sent a wide shaft of light behind them, illuminating the tunnel for nearly three hundred feet. "Can you see what it is?"

The sub began to rumble and shake. A cloud of bait fish began to swim frantically around them. Black crabs scurried to hide in the niches of the tunnel's walls. Maruul saw something emerging out of the darkness far behind them. It became thicker, glistening, until it looked like a shadow the size of a locomotive was speeding toward them.

"It's the thing!" Maruul screamed. "The fish!"

Wally's stomach did a flip-flop at the sight of the fish creature. The ganglia of its brow were swept back into tufts snapping above its head. Its mouth opened, the great slabs of cartilage parting to expose enormous, dagger-shaped teeth. The rear spotlight bounced off the creature's eyes, making the fish look like a demon barreling out of Hades.

"IT'S GOING TO GET US!" Maruul screamed.

PC opened the throttle wide. Maruul's head snapped backward from the acceleration. He turned the sub left sharply into another tunnel. The body of the monstrosity twisted, and it flicked its tail to follow. In a straightaway, PC was able to pull away, leaving the creature in darkness. He turned again and again, weaving through the network of twisting tunnels, hoping the fish would be lost.

The tunnel became dangerously congested with rocks and pinnacles. PC slowed the sub and guided it through the strange seascape. The front headlight picked up the end of the burrow—a brown, pockmarked wall of lava rock.

Maruul and Wally squirmed in their seats and stared out the Lucite shield of the cockpit. The light from the sub spilled across a cave of unbroken walls. PC turned the craft slowly until it faced out of the dead end.

"Dingoes," Wally yelled. "Dingoes."

A single VASH with a pair of dog-head killers blocked the tunnel behind them. Their ammunition canisters were empty.

"Good. They out of spears, eh," Wally said.

The dingo men slid their cockpit open. They were smiling. The rear guard leaned out clutching a steel tube.

"Not so good," PC said. "They have a torpedo hand launcher."

A small, sleek torpedo shot out of the tube, heading right for them. Its rear turbine churned the water behind it, and it closed fast. PC pushed the dive flaps down and tapped the throttle. Their sub dove as the torpedo raced overhead and hit into the dead end.

The explosion blew off the top of the lava tube, and a pressure wave tossed their sub against a rock. Chunks of stone fell.

A cloud of mud.

Sand.

The motor roared, spit out broken rotor blades, and died. PC hit the magneto switch.

Again.

And again.

The sub was dead.

"We're cornered," Maruul cried out.

"Not if that was the ocean bottom that fell in," PC said. "The blast must have opened the top of the tunnel." The dingo-head guards circled and raised the torpedo launch tube again. "We're sitting ducks," PC yelled. He grabbed the rebreathers from the floor, and passed a pair of them to Maruul and Wally. "Put them on QUICK!"

When they had their rebreathers in place, he threw open the cockpit and shouted at Maruul and Wally. "Get out!"

The three of them scrambled over each other and kicked free from the seat. PC saw the guard pointing the launch tube directly at them.

Suddenly, there was a blurring from the right, something huge and phantasmagoric shooting out from a passageway. An enormous mouth opened. There was a tumult of water and a loud snapping as enormous jaws closed on the dingo men and their sub. The torpedo gun fell, dropping into blackness as the guards' death screams cut through the water.

Maruul and Wally stared through their dive masks at the horror.

"They were just the appetizers," PC yelled into his buddy phone. "Follow me!" He thrust himself upward toward the cloud of mud. Maruul kicked after him, with Wally close behind. The visibility dropped to less than a foot. Finally, they saw an aura of light.

There was warmth.

Gases rose about them.

Higher, PC recognized the terrain of the volcano vents. He saw the narrow lode of magnesium ribboning along the ocean floor toward the reef.

"Keep coming up," PC called into his buddy phone. Maruul and Wally heard him. They broke out of the tunnel ceiling at the base of the chalk wall where Cliff had died.

"Hurry," PC shouted.

Maruul felt vibrations in the water as though an earthquake was happening.

"IT'S COMING!" she screamed.

The trio kicked and thrust out their hands to

grab at the water in front of them. They were a dozen feet from the base of the undersea white cliff when the roof of the lava tube behind them broke wide open. The huge fish crashed up through the fissure, shaking itself loose as if it was being born from the bowels of the sea.

PC reached a crevice that had been eroded into the base of the chalk wall. He slid into it sideways like a crab. The fish creature came fast. PC grabbed Maruul, pulled her under the ledge. Together they yanked Wally in with them.

The creature bit violently at the niche, trying to get at the prey. It could see them. Smell them. It turned on its side, shook its body, and thrust its arsenal of fins into the crack.

"Don't move," PC said.

Two of the creature's sharp, barbed fins swung inches from Maruul's face. The fins dug, waved frantically, and ground off chalk into a milky cloud.

"Make it go away," Maruul said. "God, please make it go away."

She heard a buzzer and felt something strange moving on her skin.

"WHAT IS THAT?" she screamed at PC.

"Change rebreathers with me," he said.

"Just tell me!" Maruul demanded. "It's some kind of automatic alarm built into the rebreather, isn't it?"

PC slid the shoot bag with Ratboy and the opals off his back. He yanked open the Velcro straps of his vest and switched mouthpieces with Maruul. "We didn't check the air supplies in the tanks," PC said. He finished slipping the shoot bag onto his back and took a couple of deep breaths.

"Take your rebreather back," Maruul said.

"Take mine, computer boy, eh," Wally offered. "I breathe too long anyway."

"No," PC said.

The fish halted its frantic tearing at the fissure. For a moment it lay still, then glided away from the cliff. It began to swim back and forth.

Waiting.

PC felt the level of oxygen in his rebreather falling with each breath. He had to breathe faster.

"I have to go up," he said.

"We can share," Maruul said, offering her mouthpiece. There was a second buzzer and vibration. A moment later, a third. All three rebreathers were running out of oxygen.

Maruul looked to PC. "What are we going to do?"

PC didn't answer. He reached his hand up to feel the ceiling of the fissure. Its whiteness came off on his hand. Maruul watched, puzzled, as PC swung the shoot bag off his back.

"What was the last part of the treasure song?" PC asked.

Maruul ran the whole of the riddle in her mind to get to the last line.

"*. . . But dawn the beast will slay,*" she said.

PC asked, "What color is dawn?"

The three of them looked at each other and then at the chalk in which they lay hiding.

"White, eh," Wally said.

PC remembered the white figures rising up through the host of monsters in the painting on the sacred wall. He reached out, grabbed a handful of the whiteness, and began to smear it onto his body.

"Help me," he said.

Wally and Maruul understood. They began to paint his hair and face with the white chalk and clay. For a moment, Maruul thought of her village. The sacred ceremonies. And Arnhem.

The trio helped each other paint their backs,

the rebreathers, and the shoot bag. Soon, they each looked like a ghost.

"What if the wisdom of the paintings is wrong?" Maruul asked.

"Believe," Wally said.

"Whatever," PC said, "you two get ready to swim for the top. And I mean that!" Maruul noticed an uncovered spot on PC's brow. She took another piece of clay and pressed its whiteness gently over it.

"We are ghosts," Wally said. "I think we be lucky ghosts."

PC saw the fish patrolling the cliff. He slid his arms up along the top of the ledge, let them curl out. The creature halted, hovered. It moved again, slowly, ten feet from the fissure.

Watching.

Smelling.

PC began to slither upright onto the whiteness of the wall until he was a phantom blended into the rest of the blazing whiteness. Maruul and Wally heard his voice in the receivers of their masks. "I don't think it can see or smell me," PC said. "Maybe the clay covers our scent, too."

PC stayed pressed into the white wall. He

crept his right hand higher, tried to pull himself up slowly. To his left, he recognized the shining strip lode of magnesium that violated the cliff. The lode was two to three feet wide in some places, a ribbon cutting down from above and across the seascape for as far as he could see. He kept his arm away from its silvery path.

Suddenly, one of his hands slipped downward in a quick motion. The creature seemed to notice. It turned and looked straight at him.

It moved closer.

Its enormous jaws stopped inches from PC's face. They opened slowly, pulling in water across its dagger teeth and expelling it through its gills. PC was face-to-face with his worst horror. The fish inched still closer, then turned away and sank back to cruise past the crack where it knew there had been food.

Wally watched the fish. He inched his way to the brink of the fissure and saw PC above him on the wall. For a moment, fear made Wally remember the safe smell of smoke. The sweet vapors of bushtucker barbecue and the warmth of a home fire. The three of them were warriors, he thought. He wanted them all to live and go back. He wanted Lightning Man and the great Rainbow Serpent to save them. More than anything, he wished he could save the sacred wall of dreaming.

He heard new sounds. A motor. Something mechanical approaching.

PC heard the sounds, too. He looked out toward the mineral towers of the volcanic vents. What appeared to be a huge metal crab with spindly, clawed legs stepped out of the curtain of gases and mineral clouds. The freakish contraption floated toward him as the fish became spooked and swam to disappear in the forest of giant seaweed.

Closer, PC saw the propeller housings protruding from the tanklike body of the vehicle. There were external floodlights. Video and still camera mounts. Remote-controlled platforms and wire baskets were tucked between its long, robotic arms. Hydraulic pincers, claws, reached forward as it neared PC. He recognized it as a DSV, a deep submergence vehicle like the United States' *Alvin* and the French *Poseidon*. He knew there were only eight or nine DSV's of this size in the world.

Dr. Ecenbarger had her own.

She stared at PC from her seat in the pressurized cockpit—a plastic bubble that rose like a Cyclops eye from the titanium of the vehicle's skin.

"Yes, the three musketeers are alive," Dr. Ecenbarger said into her mike. Her voice came through loud and clear on PC's buddy phone channel. She appeared hellish, her head glowing from the cockpit's interior of electronic screens and lighted dials. "We'll see how you do when the big fish comes back—*and it will.*"

One of the hydraulic arms shot out suddenly for PC's throat. It missed and sank into the magnesium lode, crumbling a large chunk of it. PC tried swimming for the surface, but Dr. Ecenbarger extended two long robotic arms from the vehicle. They snapped, clawed, and rotated above his head. A fourth arm with a grasper moved forward and curled around his arm to hold him tight against the cliff.

"Maruul! Wally!" PC yelled into his buddy phone. "Go for the top! Now!"

Dr. Ecenbarger looked amused in her plastic cockpit. "I heard that."

Maruul and Wally slid out quickly from beneath the ledge and started swimming up the face of the chalk wall. Dr. Ecenbarger thrust the DSV's arms out and upward to their fullest length.

"No!" PC yelled.

The claws cut into the cliff face above their heads. The doctor maneuvered the claws to force Maruul and Wally back down into the fissure.

Dr. Ecenbarger smiled. "You're all so *white*. So pure."

"Let them go," PC said.

The doctor threw a switch. A spinning drill telescoped out from the submersible, heading straight for PC. The robotic arm held him. He twisted, managed to swing his body horizontally to avoid the bore as it dug through into the cliff. The sudden motion scraped whole strips of the white clay off him. There were shallow bleeding cuts across his chest. He knew that if the fish came back, it would find him.

"I'm having trouble breathing," Maruul said. The battery in her buddy phone was drained and dying.

Dr. Ecenbarger spoke into her mike. "Let me make you and Mr. Wallygong more comfortable."

She manipulated the hydraulic arms down to the mouth of the fissure. The claws entered, snapping like hedge clippers, to seek them out. Beneath the ledge, Wally scratched at the whiteness ahead of him and helped Maruul away from the straight thrusts of the probes.

PC kicked at the steel limb restraining him. The effort consumed the last of his oxygen. He struggled to pull his arm loose as Ratboy and the stones in the shoot bag dug into his back.

"Your friends are hiding," Dr. Ecenbarger said. "We're always prepared for that." She hit a clutch in the cockpit.

With his free hand, PC slid the shoot bag around to his chest. He watched as the top section of the DSV separated from the main body. It was flat, like a stingray, less than three feet across, with its own motor and hydraulic projections. A junior robot with a screaming saw as a nosepiece. A long, thick cable tethered it to the mother DSV, as it propelled itself to the fissure and began to pulverize everything it touched. It crawled in after Maruul and Wally like a scorpion.

"Don't!" PC shouted. The doctor laughed and stepped up the power to the robot. PC punched at the cliff. He felt something sharp cutting into his hand. A crust of whiteness broke from the edge of the silvery magnesium lode.

The magnesium.

PC's hand moved across the cold metal. Magnesium that burns underwater, he thought. He heard Maruul's voice. "IT'S GOING TO GET US!"

Desperately, PC dug his free hand into the shoot bag. Dr. Ecenbarger smiled at his curious struggle. She watched him grab Ratboy and thrust the computer against the magnesium. Its thin black plastic shell broke. For a moment she thought a type of rapture of the deep had taken hold of his mind.

"What are you doing?" she asked.

He didn't answer. "Sorry, Ratboy," he whispered under his breath as he yanked the guts out of the computer. He clutched a fist of wires and circuit boards. And its *battery.*

Dr. Ecenbarger watched his actions and tried to understand. She was aware of the magnesium strip—the narrow lode of magnesium that led from the cliff to . . .

to . . .

She saw the battery sparking on the magnesium.

NO, she began to think. Then she shouted the word at PC. She pulled back the hydraulic arm that had him pinioned against the cliff. She hoped it would make him stop, but it didn't. With both hands free, he crashed the battery again into the silvery strip until it sparked.

Brighter.

Longer.

Suddenly, a white fire flared on the surface of the magnesium. The metal was burning.

Wildly.

Intensely.

The light from it was blinding, like a giant sparkler. At first, the fire began to spread along a narrow route, but then it traveled quickly along the sea bottom toward the drill tubes of the freighter. A smaller band of flames crawled up the band of magnesium toward the top of the cliff.

Three minutes, twelve seconds . . . Three minutes, eleven seconds . . .

Dr. Ecenbarger couldn't think about the dynamite planted in the opal slab of the lava tube. Her only thought now was to extinguish the blazing fuse heading beneath her freighter. She knew her entire boat with its storehouse of magnesium was a massive floating bomb.

She turned the junior robot around, made it retreat from the fissure. Maruul and Wally saw the glow of fire and followed the robot out of the fissure. PC swam toward them shouting, "Go up! Up!"

Maruul and Wally kicked, rising like ghosts on the face of the cliff. PC stayed behind and turned in place, watching for the creature.

He saw it:

The massive shadow broke out from the undulating seaweed and headed for him. PC watched Dr. Ecenbarger's arms flailing out to hit at levers in the cockpit. She sped the robot back toward its boarding niche on the DSV, its tether trailing like a macabre umbilical cord.

PC kicked hard after the robot. He managed to grasp it from the back and alter its course.

The doctor screamed, "What are you doing?"

He maneuvered the whirling saw at the front of the robot so it cut deeply into the cockpit. The plastic fractured around the doctor, water pouring in to trap her in her seat.

"Now, Dr. Ecenbarger, *you* can be the Catch of the Day," PC said.

He let go of the robot and swam back to the cliff as the shadow of the fish fell over the DSV. The creature circled for a moment above the craft. It saw the struggling doctor.

Smelled her.

EEEEEEE. EEEE.

It hurled itself downward.

PC heard the doctor scream.

Again.

And again.

The monster tore Dr. Ecenbarger loose from the cockpit like a bird of prey ripping a rodent from its hole.

For a moment, it appeared to play with her.

Savor her.

It raked its teeth along her body, causing long, scarlet incisions. Finally, it bit her in half— snapping, chewing at her lower torso until it was reduced to a shredding of blood, muscle, and bowels. Finally, it disengaged its lower jaw and swallowed all of her.

Wally and Maruul surfaced near a shallow ridge of the reef. They pulled themselves up onto a rock patch, saw the white-hot glow blazing in the deep. Men aboard the freighter saw the strip of fire heading for them. A siren screamed. Many of the men leaped overboard, shouting with terror as they tried to swim away.

The magnesium link to the freighter flared like a fuse as the fire rushed up into the hull and its storage bins. The explosion was huge. A blinding ball of white-hot fire rose high up into the sky and fractured into tremendous curving fingers of smoke. Black metal shards and debris fell everywhere. Maruul and Wally crouched until the deadly rain had stopped. There was nothing left of the freighter except a piece of burning hull.

Maruul stared at the drop-off of the chalk wall. Waves pounded against the reef as she walked to its brink. Wally stood next to her, and together they stared down into the violent water.

It seemed too long.

Much too long.

Finally, PC surfaced. At the sight of him, Maruul let out a cry of joy. Wally laughed. PC looked worn and exhausted as he swam toward them. They pulled him from the water. A smile broke out onto his face as he held high the shoot bag, with its fire opals blazing in the sun.

"The dreaming is safe?" Wally asked. "Freighter detonator kaput before it could explode the wall of dreaming, eh?"

"Yes," PC said. "The dreaming is safe."

By eight o'clock the next morning, the fog had begun to retreat from the mooring station. PC had the skiff ready and idling. Maruul and Wally prepared the breakfast. Coffee. Toast. Leftover roast turtle. They had all had time to wash up and rest. The Coast Guard had stopped by the night before to make certain they were all right.

"You saw the explosion?" Lt. Roessler asked.

"Yes," PC said. He told them about the death of his uncle on the reef. He kept it simple and called it a shark attack. There was no need to volunteer the details of what had really happened. No reason to tell the Coast Guard everything.

The sun rose in the sky behind them as they raced across the reef toward Cape Tribulation. A school of dolphins appeared off the starboard of the skiff. They began to jump across the bow and race along beside them. PC saw the marina nestled at the foot of the mountains and rain forest. Closer, he noticed there was a crowd of Aborigine women on the beach near the docks.

"What's going on?" he asked.

Maruul saw a pair of familiar beat-up old vans and a rusted purple bus parked at the edge of the sand. She recognized the faces and bright-colored skirts of the women. A single Aboriginal man with intense eyes stepped down from the bus with a mob of kids. He wore checkered shorts and a bright-yellow shirt-vest. A rifle was slung over his shoulder.

"It's my father and my twenty-seven mothers," Maruul said.

"*All* of them?" PC asked.

"Yes," Maruul said. "One father, twenty-seven mothers, and thirty-two brothers and sisters. They got the message left at the trading post—the message about Arnhem." Her family saw her and began waving as they ran along the beach toward the marina.

"Lucky guy, your papa, eh," Wally said. "Strong, too."

PC glided the skiff into its berth. He took the shoot bag out of his suitcase. Maruul lifted out the chunks of opal and cradled them in her arms. She looked into PC's eyes, then turned to

Wally. "Last night I dreamed PC and I were both *arukas*," she said. "Could that be what we're meant to be? Seekers?"

"Yes," Wally said. "You are both *arukas*."

Maruul smiled. She turned from PC and Wally and started to run toward her family. They saw her coming. They saw the happiness in her face and the crystals of fire cradled in her arms. Their faces exploded with life and her father let out a cheer. PC watched them embrace each other. He saw the laughter and love between them all. He thought of his own mother. His father. He thought of Grandma Helen standing in the vapors of burning pots. He found himself smiling. He would go home for a while, enjoy them—and show them what a real family should be.

ABOUT THE AUTHOR

Paul Zindel, who won the 1971 Pulitzer Prize for Drama for *The Effect of Gamma Rays on Man-in-the-Moon Marigolds*, once again draws upon his scientific background for *Reef of Death*. His most recent books for HarperCollins include *The Doom Stone* and *Loch*, both Recommended Books for the Reluctant YA Reader (ALA), and the tragicomic memoir *The Pigman & Me*, which *School Library Journal* said in a starred review "allows readers a glimpse of Zindel's youth, gives them insight into some of his fictional characters, and provides many examples of universal experiences that will make them laugh and cry." *The Pigman & Me* was both a 1993 ALA Best Book for Young Adults and a 1993 ALA Notable Children's Book.

Mr. Zindel lives in Montague, New Jersey.